COMRADE KOBA

BY ROBERT LITTELL

The Defection of A. J. Lewinter (1973)
Sweet Reason (1974)
The October Circle (1975)
Mother Russia (1978)
The Debriefing (1979)
The Amateur (1981)
The Sisters (1986)
The Revolutionist (1988)
The Once and Future Spy (1990)
An Agent in Place (1991)
The Visiting Professor (1994)
Walking Back the Cat (1997)
The Company (2002)
Legends (2005)
Vicious Circle (2006)
The Stalin Epigram (2009)
Young Philby (2012)
A Nasty Piece of Work (2013)
The Mayakovsky Tapes (2016)
Comrade Koba (2020)

NONFICTION
For the Future of Israel (with Shimon Peres) (1998)

COMRADE KOBA

A NOVEL

ROBERT LITTELL

THE OVERLOOK PRESS, NEW YORK

Library of Congress Control Number: 2020932378

ISBN: 978-1-4197-4832-5
eISBN: 978-1-64700-003-5

Printed and bound in the U.S.A.
10 9 8 7 6 5 4 3 2 1

ABRAMS The Art of Books
195 Broadway, New York, NY 10007
abramsbooks.com

For Banjo

"Conscience, the uninvited guest . . ."

ALEKSANDR SERGEEVICH PUSHKIN

"I don't *get* ulcers. I *give* ulcers."

COMRADE IVANOVITCH, AKA KOBA

ONE

WHERE THE KID TRIES TO SPEED UP TIME

FROM LEON'S NOTEBOOK:

THE OLD MAN: Since you're such a hotshot with numbers, kid, can you tell me how much the Soviet Union weighs?

ME: Hey, nobody can know that. It's impossible to calculate.

THE OLD MAN: Give it a stab. With its planes and tanks and ships, with its factories and machinery, with its trains and tractors and trucks, how much?

ME: An awful lot. Like, more than an awful lot. If someone could calculate the weight, it would be astronomical.

THE OLD MAN: Could an enemy of the people plotting to murder members of the politburo and restore capitalism resist the astronomical weight of the Soviet State?

ME: No way. He'd be crushed to death.

THE OLD MAN: Aaahhh, I am relieved to hear it. I sleep better knowing nobody can resist the weight of the Soviet State.

JUST THINKING ABOUT IT MAKES ME GRIN.

"Give me three reasons why I should talk to you," I remember the old man saying.

I was wolfing the ice cream he had ordered up for me at the time, two volcano-sized scoops of vanilla drenched in chocolate sauce. "My first is, I don't know who you are." I may have accidentally wiped my chin on my sleeve because he gave me one of those killer looks adults own the patent to. I didn't flinch. "My second is, since I don't know who you are, I'm not afraid of you."

I remember the old man studying me, one eye closed, one eye not, over the rim of the glass as he sipped his milk. Suddenly he sat up straight and raised his glass and toasted me the way my father used to when he drank wine and I drank pomegranate juice. Thinking about my father made me sad and I looked away, which infuriated the old man. "Goddamn it, kid, look me in the eye when I toast you, otherwise you'll have seven years of bad sex."

"Like, I'm too young to have any kind of sex," I said.

That made him smile. You could tell from the way the smile didn't fit on his lips he wasn't used to smiling. He seemed human when he smiled. Almost. Maybe that's why he didn't smile all that much. Then he said something I'm still trying to figure out. "I don't often get to talk to people who aren't afraid of me." He said this almost as if he was having the confabulation with himself. "Even Vladimir Ilyich, in the last months of his life, was afraid of me. Krupskaya, his lawful wedded codfish of a wife who couldn't warm a man's bed if her life depended on it, was terrified of me. Trotsky's great mistake was he didn't become afraid of me until it was too late to save himself."

"Who's Krupskaya? Who's Trotsky?"

He ignored my question. "I asked you for three reasons."

"I'm working on my third. Don't rush me."

HERE'S THE THING: FOR A LONG TIME GROWN-UPS who heard the story from the horse's mouth, the horse's mouth being yours truly, thought it was a fairy tale, thought I was inventing the confabulations with the old man, inventing the arrests, inventing Isabeau and the other kids hiding in the House on the Embankment, inventing the dead raincoat, inventing the secret passages between the apartments (to say nothing of the tunnel under the river Styx), inventing the big steel door with the rusted-open lock that led to the steel staircase that led to the great hall with humongous chandeliers and humongouser windows covered with window curtains so thick they suffocated sounds coming from the street I supposed was outside. Well, the laugh's on them, right? Because the editor who is publishing this book, he didn't believe me neither until I went and showed him the secret passages and the tunnel and the big steel door with the rusted-open lock.

I couldn't show him the old man because by that time he was dead and buried.

As for who the old man was, I was pretty innocent when I first climbed the spiral steel staircase to his apartment. He told me he helped run the country. He told me he was a sort of assistant tsar. He told me he personally knew esteemed Comrade Stalin. Like, I'm no longer innocent, by the way—innocence is what the old man took from me in exchange for confabulation. But hey, that's a whole other story.

Here goes nothing: It's me, Leon. The Leon who got to be friends with this old man in the last weeks of his life before he met his Maker (assuming his Maker, given the old man's awful iodine breath, was willing to meet him). The Leon who was on the listening end of confabulations with the old man, my questions fish-hooking his answers, which I scribbled on the pages of a lined notebook as soon as I got back home. The Leon who hung out with him in his apartment when nobody else could get to within shouting distance except for the comrades he called kittens, them and the household, who skimmed the marble floors of the palace in bedroom slippers so as not to wake him because it was supposed, at his age—not to mention what he might have had on his conscience being that he helped run the country—he didn't sleep all that much, which turned out to be more or less factual.

You're thinking to yourself: Like, how could the kid know a detail like that if he hadn't been there like he says he was?

I suppose I need to start at the start, the only problem being I'm not sure I can identify the start. Maybe, hey, maybe it was my dad dying of radiation poisoning. You'll probably recognize his name—David Rozental?—he was famous, here in Russia at least. He was the nuclear physicist who came up with the quantum field model of the weak nuclear force (being my father's son, I actually understand it), he was the one who convinced the general secretary it was theoretically possible to make an atomic bomb (I think that's when they gave him the Pobeda with the golf-club gear shift), later he was in charge of the super-secret Laboratory No. 2 in the Academy of Sciences and organized Russia's first chain reaction. It wasn't cooled by heavy water because Russia didn't have heavy water—they used graphite to slow down the chain. Naturally it didn't slow down and overheated. Everyone bolted except for my dad, who tried to save the precious uranium in the rods because Russia didn't have all that much uranium neither. When my dad didn't come home from work that day my mother, thinking he might have been arrested—hoping he had been arrested because the alternative was too awful—made frantic phone calls until she fell on someone at the Laboratory who told her what happened and made her swear not to say who told her. I heard my mom utter a swear word as she hung down the phone and break into hysterical sobs. Seeing her cry, naturally I cried too, though at the time I wasn't sure what I was crying about. That was four years ago, in 1949; I was six going on six and a half. David Rozental was awarded the Order of Lenin for his work on "First Lightning," which was the code name of our first Soviet atomic bomb. My mom took me with her to a secret ceremony in a stuffy hotel room filled with papier-mâché funeral flowers and stone-faced men who looked as if they were suffering from terminal heartburn. They gave me American chewing gum and a real NKVD badge. One of them, a little guy with thick heels on his shoes to make him taller and a monocle glued to his left eye, stepped up to my mother and planted a noisy kiss on both of her ashy cheeks, then permitted the back of his right hand to graze her left breast as he pinned this medal on her dress. (Hey, at six and a half I already knew about the birds and the bees.) It was in this hotel room I learned the word posthumously. Okay, let's say, for argument's sake, that was the start.

Or maybe . . . on second thought, maybe it started with my mother's arrest. Now that I think of it, that seems like a smarter place to start if for no other reason than it's fresher in my brain.

So I'll start with this major event in my life: my mom's arrest.

Thanks to my father being this important nuclear physicist, thanks to my mother being this important heart doctor in the Kremlin hospital, we'd been assigned an apartment in the House on the Embankment, on the third floor no less, where the politburo and CheKist bigwigs lived. The hero who led the storming of the Winter Palace in the glorious Bolshevik Revolution, Nikolai something or other, lived in apartment 280. I never actually saw him, my friend Isabeau did and said he had a long white beard. There was also this famous explorer, Ilya something or other, who walked the penguin he brought back from the Arctic on a leash. Him I've seen with my own eyes. The penguin was cute, the less said about Ilya something or other the better. The esteemed general secretary's cousins, the Svanidzes and the Redens, lived down the hall. I went to school with their kids—most of them were pills. The esteemed general secretary's own daughter, Svetlana, lived next to the elevator in apartment 179 with her newest husband. My chum Zinaida babysat their baby girl, which is how we heard about Svetlana having one or two husbands before the one she lived with now. The one she lived with now was named Yuri. Some of the kids whispered he was the son of A. Zhdanov, esteemed Comrade Stalin's minister in charge of weeding out rootless cosmopolitans, which us kids took to be some kind of contaminated city shrub. Once I rode down in the elevator with this Yuri guy, he stared off into space even after I said hello. I figured, like, he must have had a lot on his mind if he couldn't say hello back to a kid who wasn't supposed to know who he was.

If I climbed onto a chair, from my bedroom window of our apartment I could see the Kremlin walls, behind which the general secretary himself lived, reflected in the Moscow River flowing between the Kremlin and me on my chair looking out the window. The House on the Embankment, which was this gigantic building built long before I was born, had an awful lot of empty apartments, the doors of which were sealed with duct tape with the initials NKVD on them. I don't know why so many apartments were empty, or why even if they were empty the doors needed to be sealed with duct tape. My father, when he was still alive, would mutter something about not getting in the way of the stampede of history when I asked him to explain the duct tape. My mother would look away and scold me for asking foolish questions, the answers to which I was too young to understand. What I was too young to understand was why they didn't answer my question. I understand now. But that's a whole other story.

Weekdays I went to School No. 175, which is where all the kids living in the House went, which is how come I got to ride in a shiny American Packard driven by an actual chauffeur. There were always three or four Packards parked outside in the morning with their motors running, and the Soviet admiral moonlighting as a doorman waved me and the other kids to the one that would leave next. The House had a cinema in the minus-one basement. My best friend Isabeau said they showed American films captured by our glorious Red Army during the Great Patriotic War. I don't know how she could know that, being as us kids weren't allowed into the basement cinema. On the floor below the cinema there's a gym, a heated swimming pool, a basketball court, a laundry, and best of all a grocery store where you can buy things like Italian pasta and Cuban cigars and Scottish whisky, which was something my father especially liked. For some reason the doors to the gym and the swimming pool and the basketball court were always padlocked. There's also a cafeteria that us kids were allowed into even without parents. When my parents worked late, then after my dad died when my mom had the night shift at the Kremlin hospital, I would pick up a tin tray and point to what I wanted in the glass case, and the cook, an Uzbek with a ski-slope nose and slanty eyes, would add vegetables even if I didn't point to them and I would count out the fifteen rubles fifty to the cash register lady with the glass eye that stared off in one direction while her good eye looked disapprovingly at me. If Isabeau was there—both of her parents had been arrested, her dad executed for being a British spy even though he didn't speak British, her mother taken off to some jail or other, their apartment sealed with NKVD duct tape, but Isabeau, like me after my mother's arrest, was hiding out in our secret rooms and using the secret passageways between apartments that had been built so the House's original tenants could circulate without being seen—we would always sit at the same table, Isabeau next to me, close. She was seven and a half months older than me but she didn't have breasts yet, otherwise I would have asked if I could touch one. The people who ran the basement cafeteria never seemed to have gotten word who was and who wasn't arrested—so as long as we could pay for the food they let us eat there.

My parents didn't subscribe to *Pravda*. Like, my guess is that they were so important they didn't need to, but there was always a copy of today's paper spread-eagled in the glass case next to the admiral's pew inside the House's main door, and us kids would read the headlines while we waited for the next Packard. Which is how I found out about this doctor's plot in the Kremlin hospital.

"Did you know any of these thirty-seven terrorist doctors?" I asked my mom when I got home from school that day.

She frowned, the crinkles between her eyes making her look older than thirty-something, which is how old I think she was. "How did you hear about this?"

I told her about the *Pravda* in the glass case and the article on murderers in white coats administering harmful treatments to important members of the superstructure. "And why does the headline say the arrested doctors are Israelites?" I wanted to know.

Turned out my mother knew most of them, one actually worked in her cardiac ward at the hospital, another worked in the x-ray service on the same floor. And they were, possibly by coincidence, probably by coincidence, positively by coincidence—how could it be otherwise in esteemed Comrade Stalin's glorious Union of Soviet Socialist Republics?—almost all Israelites. Though I didn't understand why *Pravda* needed to call attention to the fact. The one or two who weren't Israelite weren't identified as Christians or Mohammedans or whatever. Likewise my dad's obituary in *Pravda* used his name in the headline—"the Soviet hero Rozental"—but didn't say he was an Israelite.

I guess that makes me one too. Israelite, not hero.

About my mom, here's what you need to know:

1. She had one of those little Chagan pistols, I think it'd been her father's during the Polish campaign after the Revolution, stashed behind some books in our secret room.

2. She owned a collection of American jazz records that she kept, along with the German gramophone and the books in English and German that my dad brought back from trips abroad, in the secret room behind the living room bookcase. You needed to reach behind *The Collected Works of I. Stalin* to trip the latch and open the door. There was a three-step stepladder in the room. If you climbed onto the top step you could see through a slit into the living room. On the living room side it looked like a crack in the plaster. It was through the slit that I watched my mother's arrest. She was sitting on the couch with the seedy cushions calmly reading a book—I knew she was making believe because she didn't have her glasses on—while the five agents, all of them wearing ankle-long raincoats even though it wasn't raining out, searched the apartment. They didn't even take their hats off inside, which is how I figured they weren't brought up all that well.

They loaded every scrap of paper they found in my father's desk, also the books in foreign languages they discovered in a pile on the floor of the toilet, also the family photo album with the photographs of arrested people missing— my mother had replaced the missing photos with others so nobody would notice the album had been *scrubbed*—into my father's old Army duffel bag. As my mom was being taken away I heard one of the NKVD raincoats ask her where her son was. "He is in Sochi with his grandmother," I heard her say. "Lucky for him he isn't here," I heard the raincoat say. "Not at all," I heard my mom say. She aimed one of those half-peeved half smiles of hers in the general direction of the crack in the living room plaster. "If he were here and witnessing this he would know I am not afraid of you. As I am a loyal Soviet citizen I have nothing to fear. He would know that with the death of his father and now my arrest, he is the man of the family and must carry on until I am released and return home." I can report that carry on after my mom's arrest is what I did. Being the man in the family, as opposed to the kid in the family, I didn't need to be reminded to brush my teeth twice a day, always using bicarbonate of soda naturally. I washed behind my ears before going to bed, I went to bed, lights out, no reading by flashlight, at nine sharp most of the time—well, make that some of the time. Hey, what's the point of being the man in the family if you can't fix your own bedtime?

3. My mom's Chagan was loaded with five bullets.

4. We argued a lot, my mom and me. She didn't understand men. She was sore at my father for dying—for putting

uranium rods ahead of her. She was sore at me for not being sore at my father for dying, also for being the spit of my father as opposed to the spit of my mother. In my defense it isn't my fault if I'm the spitting image of one parent and not the other.

5. About the arrest, I need to tell you this awful detail. After my mother had been taken away and our apartment had been sealed with NKVD duct tape, I found . . . Like, how can I explain this so you don't think it's me who's disgusting? Hey, one of the raincoats searching the rooms had deposited his calling card: a turd in the unflushed toilet. You can bet I flushed it down but the memory of this guy who couldn't— who wouldn't—flush the toilet sticks in my head. What was he trying to tell us by not flushing the toilet?

6. I don't have a number six. Yet.

On third thought, maybe I need to start off by saying how I came to know the old man, which, after all, is what this book is supposed to be mostly about. So: My mom had stashed packets of rubles tied in rubber bands in the hidey-hole behind the tiled stove. Once you knew which tile came loose, using the handle end of a spoon, it was a piece of cake to get into. Isabeau's father hid a shoebox filled with rubles in her secret room. But two, maybe three weeks after our mothers got arrested, Isabeau and me, we began running out of cash money. We would have asked for credit except the cashier lady at the cafeteria had this sign pasted on the wall behind her saying socialists don't ask for credit, them that do don't get it. For a few nights we were able to sponge money from Vladimir or Pavel or the twins' older half sister Zinaida, but that source began to dry up. We toyed with the idea of going up to the roof and fishing for pigeons, but the idea of skinning the ones we trapped and then eating the ones we skinned left the both of us appetite-less. We figured we had to take matters into our own hands, which is to say I needed to go into Moscow and sell one of the small paintings my father brought back from Paris when he attended a scientific symposium there in the 1920s. When she was instructing me on survival in case of her arrest, my mom gave me the address of Mrs. Jacobson, a lady art dealer who had a small gallery in her apartment on a side street off Gorky. Isabeau and I stopped going to School No. 175 the day our apartments were sealed off by the NKVD, so it was out of the question to just walk out the building's front door being as the admiral moonlighting as a doorman had a list of arrested people. (Isabeau once got a peep at the list, she said there were pages and pages and pages filled with names.) In the mornings the admiral used to tell anyone who asked, and some who didn't, who had been arrested the night before. Isabeau and me, we weren't supposed to be still living at the House on the Embankment. Which meant the only way I could get to the gallery with the painting was to go out the secret tunnel under the Moscow River that connected the House to the city. All of us kids knew the tunnel existed long before I'd actually gone through it. I had once wandered down there with Pavel to take a look at the round door, which opened when you spun the big wheel on it.

"I ought to go with you," Isabeau said for the tenth time, but the tone of her voice said the opposite.

"Two of us will attract attention," I said. "Besides which, this is a man's work."

"And what makes you think you're a man?"

"Your question is insulting," I told her. "My mom appointed me man of the family in her absence."

Which is how I came to go down the six flights of wooden steps at the end of our secret hallway into the minus-three basement where the tunnel began. Isabeau came with me to the round door to see me off. She ran her fingers through my hair for good luck. "Are you afraid?" she asked. Dumb question. If I was I wasn't going to admit it to a girl. "See you," I said, and with my flashlight pointing the way and the painting wrapped in newspaper stashed in my knapsack, into the tunnel I went.

Like, I'd been through the tunnel under the river (which my father, for reasons that still escape me, always called the Styx) before: the first time with my father on what he described as a "training mission," once with Vladimir and Pavel after the arrest of their parents when we went scavenging for chocolate, once with Zinaida when she went to get her ears pierced. But this was my first solo crossing. There were coaxial cables and sheaths filled with wires running along the cement wall and a film of water on the brick floor and a suffocating stale smell I associated with rotting fish or other people's farts. In the half light I could make out dozens and dozens of men camping in the tunnel, wedged into nooks, sleeping on ledges or on piled-up wooden packing crates, their thick padded Army greatcoats pulled tight around them like blankets. Hacking coughs echoed through the tunnel. There were pipes fitted with nozzles spitting thin jets of steam into the moist air, which must have been what kept the tunnels warm in winter, though it made it feel as if you were crossing through a mysterious underworld. Halfway through the tunnel a hand reached out of the darkness and grabbed my ankle as I splashed past. "Cigarette me," a man demanded, "and I'll let you go." "I don't smoke yet," I told him, jerking my foot free. He started to sob. "Knock off the noise," a voice called out angrily from the darkness, "there are comrades here trying to sleep." I reached the other end in minutes and, climbing up a steel ladder, slid open the Zhivago at the top—us kids always called the man-holes Zhivagos because the name of the industrialist who manufactured them was stamped across them. I surfaced in the park not far from the tomb of the unknown soldier. It was dark out but, unlike the darkness inside the tunnel, it was a transparent darkness, it resembled a darkness from this world and not an alternative world, and so I was, like, no longer frightened. I made my way up Gorky through masses of people hurrying home, their heads bent against a wind that wasn't blowing, at least that I could feel. I passed high-rises and medium-rises and low-rises, a lot of them with state stores on the street floors and long lines of shoppers spilling out the doors onto the sidewalk, but I couldn't tell what was for sale because there was nothing in the store windows. I reached the side street and rang Mrs. Jacobson's doorbell on the fourth house in. There was a buzz in the lock. I pushed through the door into the lobby of what must have once been the private house of a rich capitalist person. I could hear footsteps coming down the stairs even though it was carpeted. An ancient lady with an enormous shawl over her shoulders appeared. She was shorter than me but that was because she was bent like a parenthesis. I wondered if her neck ached from looking up all the time. I told her I was Anastasia Rozental's son. I told her why I'd come and unwrapped the painting. "Did your mother mention the name Amedeo Modigliani to you?" the lady asked. I shook my head. "He was a young Italian painter living in Paris," she told me. "And who is the lady in the painting?" I asked. "She is our beloved poet Anna Akhmatova," she said. "And were they so poor he needed to paint her without clothing on?" I asked. "They were young and in love," the lady said. "They were lovers. You're probably too young to know what that means." "I'm young but I'm not stupid," I said. Laughing to herself, the lady fitted on perfectly round spectacles and turned the painting over to examine the back of the canvas. "Yes, yes, three hundred rubles is the price we agreed on when I talked to your mother about selling one of her Modiglianis. Wait here, boy." The woman wrapped the painting back into the newspaper and started up the stairs with it. After a while she came down carrying a small packet. Inside the packet was a thick wad of rubles. "You can count them if you want," she said. I did want. Crouching down, I started counting, licking my thumb when it went dry and I couldn't turn the pages. I stood up and put the packet into my knapsack. "What's your name, boy?" Mrs. Jacobson asked. "Leon," I said. Peering intently at me through her spectacles, she nodded as if I had said something important. "My husband used to be named Leon," she murmured. "Isn't he still named Leon?" I asked. Mrs. Jacobson smiled the saddest smile a human ever smiled. "Where he is now he is known by a number and not a name," she said. She opened the street door. "Goodbye to you, Leon." "Goodbye, Mrs. Jacobson." I didn't really comprehend why somebody would want to be called by a number and not a name but, hey, a little birdie whispering in my ear told me it was information I didn't want to have. So I slipped out of the house and headed back to the tunnel.

The real adventure started on the return trip. I was roughly a quarter of my way into the tunnel when the beam of my flashlight hit the rusted padlock on the steel door in the arched brick wall. I kicked at the door because doors are made to kick at when, to my surprise, the rusted padlock splashed into the water at my feet and the door creaked open a crack. Not being one to back away from a challenge, I pushed it open enough to squeeze through, which is how I came to find myself in this narrow passageway that branched off from the main tunnel. The beam of my flashlight couldn't reach the end of the passageway so I naturally started down it. At the end there was a steel staircase not so rusted that I couldn't climb up, and way up at the top, at least three floors up, maybe four, there was this wooden door so narrow you had to turn sideways to squeeze through, which, me being me, naturally I did. Inside it was dark but not so dark I couldn't see that I was in this humongous ballroom-type hall the size of an airplane hangar. You could have parked two of those big Soviet bombers in it, I'm not inflating. Gigantic chandeliers dangled from a funny-shaped ceiling. Gigantic paintings of what looked like tsars and tsarinas hung on the walls. Gigantic windows were covered with curtains so thick they suffocated the sounds coming from the street I supposed was outside. (Or did I tell you this already?) I could make out four men around a table at the far end of the hangar—two in civilian suits that we kids called *forty-fivers*, because that's what men started wearing at the end of the Great Patriotic War, were standing, the two others, in Army uniforms, were sitting facing each other. There were actual rifles stacked against the wall near them. I stashed my flashlight in my knapsack and made my way across the ballroom to the table. One of the men in uniform glanced at me but didn't say anything, so I edged closer. The two men in uniforms were playing chess with the most incredible ivory chess pieces, they looked like Chinese warlords and their bodyguards. My dad taught me to play chess when I was four. He had this way of frowning if I made a dumb move; seeing his frown I would quickly take it back. I stood watching the two men in uniform for a bit. When the guy playing white moved his horse to queen's bishop six I tried to replicate my dad's frown. When the guy didn't take the hint I couldn't restrain myself. "Bad move," I said. "With a Queen's Gambit Declined, which is obviously how you opened, you need to concentrate on the king's side and not weaken the queen's side, which is what you're doing."

"The kid plays chess," one of the forty-fivers said with a snicker.

"He's right about concentrating on the king's side," the other civilian said.

The Army officer playing white, clearly annoyed, scraped back his chair and stood up. "If he's such a smart-ass, here, let him finish the game."

"Go ahead, kid," the other Army officer said. "Show the Chief how to concentrate on the king's side."

I sat down and studied the board, then moved the queen's bishop to king knight five. Black moved his rook's pawn to pawn four, attacking my bishop. I moved my rook's pawn to pawn four, offering to sacrifice my bishop. My opponent stared at the board, looked up at me, then back at the board, and with a mean smile on his thick lips ate my bishop with his pawn. My pawn ate his pawn. As black had already castled, this freed up the rook file to attack his king. Five moves later I was threatening mate along the rook file. It was about then the Army officer across from me suddenly jumped to his feet, the three others appeared to stiffen to attention. I looked behind me. An old man, throwing one hip out in front of himself and then catching up with it, was shuffling through the double door in fur-lined bedroom slippers. He was carrying a gaudy parrot in a bamboo cage in one hand and a glass of milk in the other. He was wearing rust-colored sweatpants and a brown military tunic buttoned up to his neck, which meant he'd probably been in the Great Patriotic War. There were no medals on the tunic, which meant he hadn't performed any exploits. "Who's the kid?" the old man asked.

"He wandered into the Little Corner, *Vozhd*," the Army officer playing black said. "We assumed he lives in the compound."

The old man studied me for a moment. "Do you eat your vegetables?" he demanded.

"Not when I can not," I shot back.

The old man snorted with satisfaction. "You like ice cream?" I must have nodded because he asked, "What's your favorite flavor?"

"Vanilla."

The old man snapped an order to one of the chess players: "Have Valechka bring up two scoops of vanilla drenched in chocolate sauce." He jerked his head to indicate I was to follow him and he started, very slowly, you could say almost painfully, to climb the spiral steel staircase.

The Army officer the other guy had called Chief gripped my arm and jerked me off my chair. "He's invited you up to his apartment," he said in a knife-edge whisper. He removed my knapsack and handed it to the other soldier, then patted down my arms and sides and legs. I tried to make a joke. "Like, I'm not armed," I told him. He didn't seem to think I was funny. "You'd better not be," he said, and he jerked his head in the direction of the spiral staircase. "Go."

"What about my knapsack?"

"You'll get it back on your way out."

I followed the old man up the steel steps and through a thick wooden door with sheets of steel bolted onto the inside, into an apartment. The ceiling was so low I could have touched it with my fingertips if I climbed onto a chair. The few windows I could see were slits set high in the walls and shuttered with shiny steel shutters. I passed an open door of what looked like a bedroom with an unmade bed piled with pillows. I passed two other rooms off to the left but the lights were out so I couldn't see what was in them. I followed the old man through a skating rink–sized living room—past a billiard table heaped with stacks of books—and into a smaller room that had a whopping-big desk and an old-fashioned tiled stove with long johns spread on it to dry. One entire wall was covered with posters from

American films. I taught myself American from a book my mother borrowed from the Kremlin hospital's secret library—it was called *The Catcher in the Rye*. I identified with this Holden Caulfield character so much I wound up recording my confabulations with the old man in American. Being more or less fluent in American, I was able to make out the titles on his film posters: *Abbott and Costello in Hollywood*, *The Body Snatcher*, *Lady on a Train*, *Zombies on Broadway*, to name a few. There was a papier-mâché mask of Comrade Stalin on a stand. I was relieved to see he looked very healthy, exactly like the giant poster on the side of the GUM department store on Red Square. There were books piled on the floor. Some of the book towers were so high they looked like pictures I saw of that leaning tower in Italy. I spotted some of the titles on the spines: *Peter the Great*, *Ivan the Dread*, *The Complete Works of Rosa Luxemburg*, whoever she was. There was a religious book open on the chair he waved me toward—*The Twelve Sexual Commandments of the Proletariat* by someone named Zalkind. I turned down a corner of the open page so the old man wouldn't lose his place, closed the book, and set it on the floor under the chair. On the big desk I could see thick wads of paper, each under a brick paperweight, sealed packets with NO POISONOUS ELEMENTS FOUND printed on a tag, an inkstand, a bottle of Borzhom water, a pipe rack with four or five pipes in it, a black telephone, and a very big revolver. The old man set his parrot down on the floor and, sinking with a sigh into the soft chair behind the desk, started to sip his milk. "You probably have a name," is what I remember him saying.

Light from the desk lamp gave me a good look at his face. I need to say it was one heck of a face. His hair was a dirty grey that didn't come from not washing regularly and was thinned out to where it only covered half his scalp. The part of the scalp I could see was stained with reddish blotches. His face was full of pox scars, his bulging bullfrog's eyes had teabags under them, the lids blinked so rapid-fire fast over the watery whites of his eyes it made me think he was trying to wash away unpleasant thoughts before they could infect his brain. There was a single black hair escaping from his left nostril, tufts of hair on the lobes of his ears, a dead sprig of a mustache on his upper lip, crumbs of white foam at the corners of his mouth, a turkey's sack of sagging skin under his chin. And he, excuse the expression, passed gas a lot. As he wasn't embarrassed I figured I oughtn't be neither so we just went on talking as if nothing had punctuated the confabulation. As for his teeth, all I can say is he badly needed the address of a good dentist. I could see the old man was wearing cloves of garlic on a string around his neck. His left hand, toying with one of the cloves, looked crippled, the fingers didn't seem to work all that well. Maybe it was my imagination but his left arm seemed shorter than his other arm. "Everyone has a name," I managed to say. "Mine's Leon. My father was a big admirer of esteemed Comrade Stalin and decided, if I turned out to be a boy, which as you can see I did, to name me after him. My mother wanted to name me after her dead father. The dead father won. What's yours?"

"That depends."

"On what?"

"It depends on who's speaking to me and how far back I go with them. My sainted mother called me her little Soso. The workers in the Putilov factory in Petrograd knew me as Comrade Ivanovitch. I was Chichikov in a more gentrified suburb of the city. I snuck into Vienna using a passport with the name Stavros Papadopoulos. My Georgian friends, the few I have left, the few who weren't executed, call me Koba, which was my *nom de guerre* in the roaring Caucasus before the Revolution. The original Koba was a brigand in a popular Georgian novel that I never read, to tell the truth. I was too busy making history to read history. You can call me Koba."

I tried it on for size. "Koba. Fine. Does your mom live here with you?"

"She passed away before you were born," he said. His eyes turned into slits and he studied me through them. "You ask a lot of questions for a kid. What do you do?"

"I used to go to school. Right now I'm more or less on vacation. When I went to school I was the editor of my Young Pioneer newsletter."

"Which makes you a journalist."

"My father called me his little journalist."

"I have an idea. Why don't you interview me? You ask questions. I'll answer the ones that don't give away state secrets."

"What kind of questions?"

"Whatever comes into your head. If you ask enough questions and write down my answers when you get home, you'll have an authorized biography."

I figured it was no skin off my nose if he wanted me to write his biography, authorized or un-. Maybe he was important enough people would be interested in his answers. Maybe not. Either way what did I have to lose except time? So I started off with "I noticed you speak Russian with an accent. How come?"

"Ha! The kid's got an ear for language. I was born in Georgia, in a cesspit of a town called Gori. I went back there last year, or was it the year before? I didn't recognize the town. The banks of the river I used to swim in were filled with factories. I found my old house—I knew it was my old house because my mother marked my height in the doorjamb every year on my birthday. Funny thing is, I don't remember being that short."

"If you're Georgian, that means you're not Russian."

"Napoleon wasn't French. Hitler wasn't German. I'm not Russian, by birth at least. What of it? Given my father's Ossetian-Georgian roots, you wouldn't be wrong if you thought of me as vintage Georgian wine bottled in Moscow." He laughed at his own joke. "That's pretty good—vintage Georgian wine bottled in Moscow! Remember the phrase, kid. Write it down when you get back home. It could be the subtitle of my authorized biography."

"Besides the language, besides the accent when you speak Russian, is there a difference between Russians and Georgians?"

"Is there a difference between day and night? The Russians I know are hard put to remember the names of their great-great-grandparents. A Georgian, if he prides himself on being a man, can identify, by baptismal name and patronym, his ancestors back eight generations. When two Georgians meet for the first time they talk genealogy. Given how small the country is, chances are they'll find a common ancestor. One man's great-grandmother's aunt was a cousin of the other man's mother's uncle's wife's great-grandmother."

"My grandparents on my father's side are all dead. So is my father."

I don't think he heard me, or if he did I don't think he cared about me as much as he cared about himself. "I spoke Georgian long before I spoke Russian," I remember him saying. "I didn't speak Russian fluently until I enrolled in the seminary to become a priest. Those long dark beards on the faces of religious men, they're a kind of mask. All you see is the eyes peering out at you. The peasants have a saying, *A beard is worn even by goats.* How I love to shave—shaving every morning is an animal pleasure. The scratching sound the straight razor makes on my skin is music to my ears. Being beardless reminds me that I escaped from all that seminary shit."

"So you're not a priest?"

He snorted through his nose, which came across as a kind of bugle call. "We used to say: You were welcomed into the church for what you believed, you were banished from the church for what you knew. I was banished from the Tiflis seminary for what I knew, which is that god the father dispatching his only son down to earth to suffer excruciating execution for the original sin of Adam, which according to the sex-obsessed Augustine was lust, is a fairy tale. It didn't help my case with the abbot that I was preaching the gospel according to Marx in my spare time."

"What is the gospel according to Marx?"

"History repeats itself, the first time as tragedy, the second time as farce."

"I'm not sure I understand—"

"You will when you grow up. Where was I? I was telling you about the seminary. To her dying day my old mother, may she rest in peace, wished I'd taken priestly vows. In a manner of speaking, I did take their goddamn vows. In a manner of speaking, I am a priest. Like Stalin, I listen carefully to confessions. I devise appropriate punishments to help guilty individuals come to terms with their crimes. Ha! You would not go wrong thinking of me as a kind of philharmonic conductor who orchestrates people's lives." He tugged at the lapel of his military tunic. "Coincidentally, I happen to hold the rank of generalissimo."

"I noticed your tunic. My father had one just like it when he went off for his month of Army reserve. I noticed there are no medals on your tunic . . ."

"I am a modest person—unlike some of Stalin's polit-buro kittens, who wear their medals to bed, I keep mine in a shoebox." There was a speck of laughter in his eyes now. "Listen, I take my cue from Stalin himself, who is the person-ification of modesty—when his kittens proposed renaming Moscow *Stalinodar*, he flatly refused. I bet they don't teach that little detail in your school."

I remember the old man was puffing away on one of his cigarettes when out of the blue he asked me, through the smoke, if I believed in god. I told him I was agnos-tic like my father. "Do you know what agnostic means?" he demanded.

"Not really," I admitted. "I think it's someone who is afraid to believe in god and afraid not to believe in god. What about you? Do you believe in god?"

"That Teutonic holy man Luther, who was excommunicated at the Diet of Worms for his troubles, hit the bull's-eye when he nailed his thesis to the door of a cathedral: the church is a brothel the popes who run it fart devils. When I was young and more or less was afraid not to believe in god, as you put it, I was furious at the metropolitan who presided over my seminary for pretending this god of his was righteous. Righteous, my ass! Which is how I came to worship the fallen angel we identify as Satan. It was Satan who crafted Adam and Eve naked in Eden and tempted them with original sin to irritate god the father. I do my damnedest to irritate god the father whenever I can." The old man, nodding as if he agreed with what he had just said, seemed quite pleased with himself. "Back in my brigand days, in Georgia, I thought life had a hidden meaning and I was determined to find it. I thought history was bent out of shape by heroes and I was determined to become one. Which, now that I think of it, is probably how I stumbled across Communism and V. Lenin, the pilot fish leading his school of Marxist sea turtles to revolution. Listen up, kid, don't repeat what I am about to tell you to anyone while I'm still alive."

"I won't," I promised. And I kept my word. But now that he's dead I can say what he said.

"I'm not convinced history is bent out of shape by heroes," is what he said. "I'm not convinced life has any meaning other than death."

I wasn't sure if he was kidding. I wasn't sure if he wasn't. I would have asked him, except a woman, who looked to be roughly the same age as my mom give or take a year or three, appeared in the doorway. She was wearing a long white kitchen apron and carrying what turned out to be a bowl of ice cream. The old man nodded in my direction. She came over and with a very gentle half smile that reminded me of my mom's half smile handed it to me. "Would you like another glass of warm milk, Joseph?" she asked. "Not tonight, Valechka," he growled, waving her away with the back of the hand he didn't keep buried in a pocket of his tunic. The old man and the woman in the apron looked at each other for a long moment as if a secret message was passing between them. "Come to bed, Joseph," she said softly. "You have a big day tomorrow." She turned to leave.

"In a while—for once I have an interesting visitor," the old man called after her. "Close the door on your way out."

"I always close the door on my way out," she called back. "I always open it on the way in," she said. And I heard her add with a soft laugh, "I'll come back when the boy is gone."

"Is she your wife?" I asked when the door clicked closed behind her.

I could see my question vexed the old man. "She is my housekeeper, period," he said. His nostrils flared the way my dad's nostrils flared when he wasn't sure how far to go answering my questions about girls and love and marriage and making babies. Little did he know I knew the answers before I asked the questions. I asked them because I got a kick out of watching his nostrils flare.

I dug into the ice cream. It was lip-smacking scrumptious. "You must be very rich to live over a palace," I remarked.

"As a matter of fact I am what you might call very rich. My desk drawers are filled with rubles, wads of them tied up in rubber bands, but I never use money myself. I don't have to." He must have spotted the doubt in my eyes because he reached into one of the drawers and pulled out a thick wad of rubles to show he hadn't made it up. "You need some money, kid?" When I looked uncertain, he said, "Here, take the money—it won't bite you," he said, tossing the packet over to me.

Like, I wasn't going to say no, was I? "But you must need your rubles to pay for food," I said, pocketing the ones he gave me before he could change his mind. "You need to pay rent for this apartment—"

He snorted through his nose again, which I took to be his way of saying he didn't pay for food, he didn't pay rent for the apartment.

I looked around. The old man's flat was big, easily twice as big as ours in the House on the Embankment. It must have been a hundred fifty square meters at least, which meant, under Soviet law, it needed to be a collective apartment. "So where are the others who live here?"

"There are no *others* living here. I live alone."

"You don't share the kitchen, the bathroom with another family?"

He only smiled that twisted smile of his.

"Do you work in Moscow?"

"I suppose you could say that I work in Moscow."

"Do you go to an office?"

"Where I am is the office."

"What exactly do you do?"

"My mother put the same question to me before she went the way of all flesh. I'll tell you what I told her. I organize the disorder, I disorder the organized, and in the process I manage to separate the good apples from the bad apples." When I looked puzzled he added, "That's a metaphor. It's another way of saying I am an assistant tsar—I help run the country."

"If you help run the country you must know esteemed Comrade Stalin."

My question seemed to tickle Koba. "I suppose you could say that. Yes, in a manner of speaking, I do know your esteemed Comrade Stalin."

"Does he look like the giant portrait of him on the side of GUM?"

"He's gotten older. The portrait hasn't."

"So what's he like?"

I remember him staring over my head, that horizon look in his eyes, the kind of look I'd spotted in my father's eyes when they could still see, when he was still alive, when he was trying, without success, to convince my mother we should all move to Germany, where he'd been offered a teaching post at a university, which would have meant I would have grown up speaking German as well as Russian and American.

"Where was I?" the old man muttered. "Ah, yes, you want to know what your esteemed Comrade Stalin is like. He carries the weight of the world on his shoulders, which probably explains why his shoulders sag. He doesn't sleep nights, worrying about the next war with the capitalist imperialists. The thing he's proudest of, he has been known to boast about it to his politburo kittens, is he solved the peasant problem by creating farming collectives manned by a new breed of agricultural proletarians. They said it couldn't be done, they said the fucking peasant—the last capitalists in Soviet Russia—would never give up their two precious cows and miniscule vegetable gardens, they said the pricks would kill their cows and burn their grain before giving them to a collective, they said the result would be a massive famine."

"So what happened?"

"So what happened was some hundred and twenty million peasants were shoe-horned into collective farms. The poor sapskulls who resisted the collectives were sent packing to hell."

"Were they right about the massive famine? Was there not enough to eat?"

"If you're going to be a journalist, you need to ask the right question. The right question is *was there more to eat than before?*"

"And? Was there?"

"That depends."

"On what?"

"On whether you get your information from the anti-Soviet propaganda polluting the capitalist press or the honest articles in our own Socialist press."

"What else is esteemed Comrade Stalin proud of?"

"He's a smart cookie, our Stalin. He invented Stalin slices to make the bread supply feed more factory workers in the cities. Ah, and he added a clause to the 1934 Soviet Penal Code making homosexuality a crime, which put him in the good graces of the patriarch of the Russian Orthodox Church. He also takes credit for protecting Lenin's Revolution and the great Socialist experiment from the saboteurs who would have brought back capitalism."

From his bamboo cage on the night table, the parrot echoed the old man's word in a cawing screech. *"Rev-oh-lou-shun, rev-oh-lou-shun."*

"The list of Stalin's achievements is as long as my good arm. Longer even. After the Revolution, Lenin couldn't work up the nerve to execute the tsar and his family. Stalin had to talk him out of putting the tsar and the whore of a tsarina on trial, in which case he would have been able to execute the tsar and his wife but not the tsarevich and the daughters. Stalin convinced him a public trial would be risky. We Bolsheviks had to get rid of the Romanovs once and for all so there would be nothing left of the royal line around which the Whites, who were waging civil war to destroy our Revolution, could rally."

The old man swivelled his chair one complete turn, as if he was winding himself up. "What year are we?" he suddenly demanded.

"We're the middle of February, 1953."

"Listen up, kid, sixty-four years from now—in 2017—the Revolution will be one hundred years old. If the goddamn capitalists have triumphed, if the glorious Union of Soviet Socialist Republics has been consigned to the dustbin of history, to use Trotsky's picturesque phrase, you just know the fucking historians will blame it all on Joseph Stalin. *Stalinism*, they'll shout from the rooftops, *was not Communism!* But any idiot can see that Stalinism was the ultimate manifestation of Communism. Stalinism was the only way to save the Bolshevik Revolution from the muddle the egghead Lenin created." He laughed the way I imagine a maniac being buckled into a straitjacket would laugh. Tears squirted from his eyes. Saliva accumulated in a corner of his lips. "Russia being Russia," he gasped when he had caught his breath, "the day will come when there will be a nostalgia for the Joseph Stalin who saved the Revolution. Who understood, like Thomas Aquinas, that evil exists in mistaking means for the end. Stalin never made that mistake—long before he set eyes on Lenin he understood that means was the seed, ends was the tree. Even if he never achieves it in his lifetime, Stalin never lost sight of the tree—a utopia called Communism. As the peasants say, one generation plants the trees, the next profits from the shade."

"*Rev-oh-lou-shun, rev-oh-lou-shun.*"

"What's with the parrot?"

"Our miners in the Donbass take canaries down with them into the mines. It's an early warning system. If the air is poisoned the parrot is the first to kick the bucket. One of my guards, a brave fellow from the Donbass, had the idea I'd be safer if I had a parrot. I've become attached to him. He's called Kyril Modestovich. That's the name of the parrot in Pasternak's revolting book our security organ confiscated, though the son of a bitch obviously has other copies stashed around the city because he's been reading chapters aloud to friends for years. You've probably heard of this Pasternak fellow. He's Israelite, by the way. His name was in the newspaper when it turned out he'd been working off and on since the 1920s on an anti-Soviet book about some doctor."

"My father said something about Pasternak once but my mother shushed him, I don't know why. I take it you're not in love with this Pasternak—"

"I have a soft spot in my heart for the prick. Maybe it's because he translated my favorite Georgian poet, T. Tabidze, before Tabidze was executed for anti-Soviet activities. When I was younger I used to be able to recite entire poems by Tabidze. *Heavenly color, color blue* was one of my favorites. Now that I'm getting on in years I remember a line or two here, a line or two there. Maybe it's because Pasternak himself is a poet and I have a soft spot for poets. You wouldn't know it to look at me now, kid, but I used to write poetry myself. I wasn't all that much older than you when I wrote my first poems. Several of them were published in *Iveria*, that's a newspaper in Georgia, though as I was on the tsar's 'most wanted' list I didn't sign my real name. I published under the pseudonym Soselo, which was another of my mother's pet names for me."

I asked him what kind of poetry he wrote.

"Why, love poems, what else? Why would a poet write anything but love poems? It was a surefire way to sweet-talk a girl into your bed. You know about sweet-talking girls into bed, don't you?"

"Hey, Koba, I'm only ten and a half."

"You attracted to girls yet?"

"Not in the way you mean. Not yet. But I will be in a year or two."

I can hear the old man's laughter ringing in my ear as I describe this confabulation. "Why wait?" is what I remember him saying.

"Like, don't rush me, huh," is what I think, knowing me, I would have replied.

I could tell the old man was enjoying the confabulation. "Listen, in Siberia, where I've been seven times—I'm not making this up: *seven fucking times!*—sweet-talking a girl into your bed was a matter of life and death more than sex, it was a matter of staying warm enough to live through the night, of surviving minus forty until the morning when the temperature rose to a reasonable minus twenty." Koba shut his eyes and breathed musically through his nostrils. "In Solvychegodsk, a miserable godforsaken collection of huts that passed for a village in the Arkhangelsk Oblast, I fell madly wildly frantically in lust with a schoolgirl, her name was Pelageya Onufrieva, we spent most of the winter clinging to each other in a narrow bed with a sheepskin rug for a blanket. Which is how we managed to survive when the mercury in the thermometer outside our window froze. When the ice thawed, so did my lust for Pelageya."

I wasn't sure how I was supposed to react to these intimate details he was laying on me so I decided to change the subject. "Your poems must have been pretty gosh darn good if they were published," is what I said.

Koba rose to his feet behind the desk and, straightening his shoulders and thrusting out his good arm, declaimed lines from a poem I presumed he had written before he became an old man.

I'll bare my breast to you, extend
My arm in joyous greeting, too.
My spirit trembling, once again
I glimpse before me the bright moon.

I had no inkling what you could say to a poet about his poetry without being rude. From the way he looked at me I know he expected me to say something. Here's what I remember coming out with: "Your parents must have been very proud of you."

"My father, who was a first-class prick, considered poets to be fairies and poetry a waste of time," the old man said, sinking back into his desk chair. "He couldn't read, he couldn't even sign his fucking name. He had his fleeting moment of glory when the last prince in the Caucasus, Simeon Amilakhvari, who lived in a revolting palace above Gori, showed up at the shop of the only cobbler in town, the drunken Besarion Jughashvili. I remember being sent to fetch a small rug so His Serene Highness wouldn't have to set his royal stocking on the dirt floor while Besarion repaired his boot. When my father wasn't sober enough to repair boots he would whip me for misdeeds he assumed I was guilty of. Once, you're not going to believe this, kid, he beat me for biting my nails, the next night, dead drunk, he beat me for not biting my nails. You probably think I'm making this up."

"Not at all. Not at all."

"I'm not making it up. I don't want to leave you with the impression it scarred me for life, this kind of thing happened all the goddamn time in Gori. It was a backwater. Ha!

Nobody there ever heard of the Jew Freud. My father was a son of a bitch but his father was a son of a bitch before him. So my father did to me what his father did to him. If my sainted mother tried to get in his way, she got the back of his hand. She wanted me to become a priest so I could get absolution for crimes she was sure I was going to commit. When she visited me in Moscow, she was worried sick there was no longer a tsar to keep Russia from sinking into chaos. She asked me what I did for a living. I told her what I told you—I help run the country. She didn't even try to mask the disappointment in her eyes. For her it was a priest or nothing."

It was long about then the old man lugged a thick silver pocket watch from the breast pocket of his medal-less tunic. Having been raised by parents who went to great pains to teach me social skills, I identified this as a hint and made my excuses, mumbling the old saw about it being way past my bedtime. Laughing under his breath, the old man said something about it being way *before* his bedtime. I need to report I almost didn't make it past the bodyguards down below in the bomber hangar. Hefting my knapsack, the one they called Chief said, too quietly for comfort, "That's a lot of money you have in your sack—where the hell did you get it?" I was in a panic to think what I could possibly say when the old man appeared at the top of the spiral staircase. "Is there a problem?" he demanded. "No problem, *Vozhd*," the Chief replied quickly. "I enjoyed our conversation, kid," the old man called down to me. "I got a kick out of being interviewed by you. The adult journalists who interview me barely scratch the surface. They're afraid to ask questions that are too personal." He saluted me with his good arm. "Come back to the Little Corner anytime."

I saluted him back. "Count on me," I said as I liberated my knapsack from the Chief.

Looking back over my shoulder as I crossed the hangar I noticed the housekeeper, the lady the old man called Valechka, making her way up the spiral staircase. She was wearing a man's long white nightshirt. With the light behind her it was a bit transparent. Having been raised by parents who went to great pains to teach me social skills, you can bet I looked away fast and didn't jump to conclusions.

TWO

WHERE THE KID SEES HIMSELF AT TWENTY-FIVE

FROM LEON'S NOTEBOOK:

THE OLD MAN (*getting up from his desk*): I need to piss.

ME: You just did.

THE OLD MAN: It's my fucking prostate.

ME: Who's that?

THE OLD MAN: It's a gland men have and women don't.

ME: Maybe you ought to see a doctor.

THE OLD MAN: The good doctors are all Jews. Most of them have been arrested for thinking anti-Soviet thoughts.

ME: Like, how can you know what someone's *thinking?*

THE OLD MAN: It's the business of our CheKists to know what people are thinking. One day they're thinking anti-Soviet thoughts, the next they're plotting to poison Stalin.

ME: Hey, you're paranoid enough to make a good chess player. There has got to be one doctor left in Moscow who can repair this prostate of yours.

THE OLD MAN: Listen, even if there was one who hasn't been arrested, Gehenna will freeze over before I let a Jew doctor stick his finger up my asshole and examine my prostate.

REMEMBER THE OLD MAN SHAKING HIS HEAD IN frustration the second time I visited him. "When I invite Stalin's politburo kittens to supper," he said, "we run out of conversation by dessert and I end up showing them one of those American movies our soldiers found in Hitler's Berlin bunker. Turns out Hitler had a weakness for American films. Ha! Maybe the *Führer und Reichskanzler* and Goebbels and Göring and Speer also ran out of conversation by dessert! Mind you, even an American movie you've seen four or five times is better than being alone with your thoughts when the guests run out of conversation after a late supper. With you, I don't seem to run out of conversation. That's what I like about your visits, kid—I don't need to see a movie into the early hours of the morning to fill the silence with noise."

"What I like about talking to you," I hear myself telling him, "is I find out things I didn't know I knew."

I remember him lazily swivelling his chair around so that he could see himself in the oval mirror on the wall behind the desk. He sat there gazing at his reflection with what, remarking his cat's eyes and flaring nostrils in the mirror, I took to be despair. Hey, in his defense, it can't be cool to look as old as you actually are. (I'm not cool about looking as young as I actually am.) I heard him clear his throat, which meant words must have been working their way from his brain to his lips. "In my mind's eye," I heard him say, "I'm still the twenty-five-year-old brigand in Georgia, always one jump ahead of the pricks in the tsarist constabulary, never sleeping in the same bed two nights in a row, never screwing the same girl two nights in a row, robbing banks and sending valises stuffed with rubles to Vladimir Ilyich to finance his half-baked harebrained revolution. What I bring to Lenin's table isn't the bleeding heart of the revolutionist but the peasant's festering hatred of the fucking tsar and the army of kleptocrats who kiss his royal ass. People I pass on the dirt streets of Gori identify with this hatred, which is why they bow from the waist and call me *batono*, which is Georgian for *sir*. I have these two beautiful pearl-handled revolvers tucked into my waistband and an erection five times a day, I skinny dip in the muddy Liakhva with one of my sweethearts, or two, we dry ourselves with sunshine, when I ask what they're wearing under their dresses they answer *perfume*. I have a full head of unmanageable hair and a flamboyant mustache that tickles the girl's cunt when I spend the night with one of them. Those were the halcyon days! I'm not embarrassed to say it was exhilarating to be a revolutionist—it was a way of putting my rage against my birth father and my imperial father Nicholas II to good use, it was a way of escaping the excruciating dreariness of day-in, day-out life in the Caucasus. Looking back . . . Looking back I think it was the only time in my life I was really happy to be alive. I knew *who* my enemies were. I knew *why* they wanted me dead. And I took a certain satisfaction—a certain *pleasure* even—in killing them before they could kill me. All that changed with the Revolution and we Bolsheviks became the permanent residents of the Kremlin. People still bowed from the waist and called me *khozyain,* which is Old Russian for *master,* but I doubt it was meant as a sign of respect. As Stalin has instructed us, survival depends on identifying *potential* enemies and cutting them off at the knee before they become active enemies. I still kill my enemies before they have a chance to kill me, but, much as I hate to admit it, the pleasure has worn thin. If I'm still alive, it's because I follow Stalin's golden rule to the letter: *Trust no one. Keep an eye on your wife, keep your enemies close, keep your friends closer.* I kept Trotsky, the stinking Jew intellectual in love with his own voice, close. I kept Zinoviev and Kamenev and Bukharin closer. That's how I found out the bastards were scheming to have Stalin's skin—all three, caught in the act, were sentenced to the Highest Measure of Punishment. Ha! Bukharin, just before they shot a bullet into the nape of his neck, asked for pencil and paper and scribbled a note to Stalin. *Why do you need my death?* I'll wager my last ruble they don't teach that little detail in your school. As if the fucker didn't know *why* Stalin needed his death. At his public trial in the Trade Union House, which Stalin watched from a secret window in the back, he pled guilty to plotting to murder Soviet leaders and restore capitalism in Russia. The peasants say there is no evil without a grain of good in it. In Bukharin's case I looked carefully for the grain of good. There was none to find. I kept his pencil-written *memento mori* under my blotter for years. I would read it before going to bed in the expectation of sleeping more soundly knowing the fate of Stalin's enemies."

The old man blinked rapidly, as if he was washing away a disagreeable memory. "Where was I? Ah, I was telling you about the two pearl-handled revolvers tucked into my waistband. You familiar with erections, kid? You know what part of a girl is the cunt?"

I knew, thanks to my dad, about erections, though I'd never had an actual one myself. Yet. Girl anatomy was a different story but I wasn't about to tell Koba that. "Come on," I said with a whine I had perfected when my mom would ask me if I'd done my homework. "Like, I wasn't born yesterday."

"You can learn a lot about girls from me, kid."

"Such as?"

"Such as steer clear of the ones that sit with their two feet planted flat on the ground. You want to get to know the girls who cross their legs. When girls cross their legs, even if they don't know it, they're masturbating. You familiar with masturbation?"

Fact is, I'd never masturbated. Yet. And now that I thought about it I realized Isabeau usually sat with her legs crossed. But I wasn't about to share intimate personal details with an old man with iodine breath so foul you needed to sit upwind from him. I tried to change the subject. "Hey, my dad would sometimes say to me, you're telling me more than I need to know. Talking to you makes me understand what he meant."

I'm not sure he heard me. "Reality rears its ugly head when I look at myself in a mirror," the old man rambled on, studying his reflection in the mirror, talking to his reflection, not to me. "I stare at this old man staring back at me but the god-awful truth is I don't recognize him. He's a complete stranger. He's from a foreign country. He's from another planet. He's not the me I was and in my mind's eye still am. How the hell did I get to be seventy-four? Why didn't time slow to a crawl when I ordered it to?" His eyes suddenly focused on the me that was in the mirror. "What do you see when you look in a mirror, kid?"

"I see myself at twenty-five. I see myself with a flashy mustache that tickles the girl's upper lip when you kiss her. I see myself letting the back of my hand graze her breasts if she's old enough to have breasts. Like, I can't wait to be twenty-five. Grown-ups don't get that being ten and a half isn't a stroll across a field. People pat you on the head and tell you to have a happy childhood, as if a happy childhood vaccinates you against an unhappy adulthood."

The old man raised his good hand, the way we kids did at school, hoping to get a word in. "It's an *unhappy* childhood that vaccinates you against an unhappy adulthood. I'm speaking from personal experience."

"Either or, for me it's too late to have a happy childhood. I used up the happy part of my childhood when my dad died protecting uranium rods. I used up the rest of my childhood worrying about whether I'd survive childhood. I hate myself for being too young and letting so many people boss me around. I need to be twenty-five as soon as possible. If only I could figure out how to speed up time."

THREE

WHERE THE KID DISCOVERS WANTING TO BE LIKED IS A FATAL HANDICAP

FROM LEON'S NOTEBOOK:

THE OLD MAN: You smoked a cigarette yet?

ME: No.

THE OLD MAN (*holding out a lighted cigarette*): Want to try?

ME: My mom will kill me if she finds out.

THE OLD MAN: What she doesn't know won't kill her.

ME (*cautiously puffing on the old man's cigarette*): I'm thinking seriously of giving up cigarettes.

THE OLD MAN (*exasperated*): Not like that, kid. Breathe in. Suck the goddamn smoke into your lungs.

I try again and wind up with a coughing fit that almost makes me vomit. The old man thinks my distress is hilarious.

I T WAS ISABEAU WHO EXPLAINED THE DOCTORS' plot to me, which is to say explained there was no plot, period, none at all, nothing. The arrested doctors had been practicing medicine, not conspiring to murder the esteemed general secretary and other members of the government. Isabeau's dad, the thing I remember most about him being the way his mustache twitched when he tried not to laugh, worked as a chemotherapist at the Kremlin hospital before being executed as a British spy. Her mom received a form letter announcing the execution. She was invited to collect his personal belongings and pay for the bullet that had been shot into the back of his neck. Which is how Isabeau came to hear about the doctor's plot. A week or so after her mother paid for the bullet, Isabeau, her ear glued to the secret door leading to her apartment, listened to *her* mom being arrested. She could hear her pleading with the agents who had come to get her, it was just before sunup, while they turned their rooms inside out—or should I say outside in?—looking for whatever they were looking for. Which they didn't find, according to Isabeau. No letters from abroad, no books in British, no shortwave radio to listen to the BBC, no photographs of her executed father palling around with British diplomats, no pistols loaded with poisoned bullets, no scalpels coated with strychnine, no syringes filled with bubonic plague. Isabeau, it goes without saying but, hey, I need to say it all the same, was scared out of her skin—she ran down the secret hallway that connected our apartments to my secret room and, squatting in a corner, shivering as if it was winter inside as well as outside, began to cry. Silently. A waterfall of tears spilled from her eyes, trickled down her cheeks, soaking into the starched collar of her starched dress, but no sound escaped her lips. None. These tears without sound are what scared me. It took a while before she was able to speak without hiccupping and tell me what happened. Her mother, who, like my mom, worked in the Kremlin hospital, was the dietician in charge of providing meals to patients, she had been arrested the same night as my mother but a few hours later. Maybe it was the same guys who, once they had locked my mom up in jail, came back for Isabeau's mom before the sun came up. Now that I think of it, it must have been the same guys because Isabeau also found a turd in the toilet after her mother was taken away. Hey, factory workers work on a quota—they're expected to manufacture a certain number of, say, left shoes on a twelve-hour shift—so who's to say those NKVD raincoats didn't also have a quota: so many apartments searched, so many incriminating documents confiscated, so many turds deposited in the suspects' toilets, so many doctors known to be planning to murder the general secretary arrested on any given night shift.

About Isabeau, here's what you need to know:

1. She argued a lot with her dad, obviously before he was executed. He didn't understand women, even ones who were too young to have breasts. He thought kids were furniture—they needed to be seen but not heard. He thought his wife needed to be like one of those artsy paintings hanging on the wall. Which only made Isabeau's voice shriller when she tried to educate him about something she called female-ism, which she described as a work badly in need of progress.

2. She is more street-smart than me but I know more than her, starting with differential calculus, starting with Einstein's general theory of relativity, starting with my dad's quantum field model of the weak nuclear force.

3. She was christened Isabeau after a namesake, her French grandmother, a gutsy aristocrat who, breaking with her family, ran off to join the glorious Bolshevik Revolution and died of starvation in 1942, during the nine-hundred-day German siege of Leningrad, when she couldn't bring herself to eat the rats her daughter bought on the black market. Grandma Isabeau's medals, from the Revolution, from the Great Patriotic War, are displayed on a velvet cushion in a glass case in granddaughter Isabeau's bedroom, though they didn't save her son-in-law from execution or her daughter, the rat aficionado, from arrest, did they?

4. She is incapable of faking being polite so she sometimes rubs people the wrong way, which explains how come she doesn't have all that many friends outside of the friends she already has, starting with me, the twins Vladimir and Pavel, and their half sister, Zinaida, who lisps when she's tired. Isabeau likes me best, she thinks I'm cute, she's always running her fingers through my hair to check if I've washed it and (her not-so-funny joke) to kill the gnats if I haven't. Sometimes she exhales onto the thick glass of my eyeglasses and cleans them for me with the hem of her dress, sometimes I catch a peep of her underpants when she does this. She puts up with the other kids from the sealed apartments who we hang out with because, as Isabeau said when she explained the facts of life to me, company makes misery feel less miserable, or words to that effect. I don't know for a fact that she's wrong. I'm not positive she's right.

5. With her father dead and buried in a mass grave god knows where and her mother off in jail somewhere, Isabeau got into her mom's makeup and started using kohl on her eyelids, black nail polish on her fingers and toes and purple lipstick that makes her look eleven going on twenty-five. (Maybe that's her way of speeding up time.) She also listens to American songs on a little machine her father brought back from the Soviet sector of Germany, which I think is against the law—I'm talking about the songs, not the machine. I'm not sure who Big Mama Thornton is but if "Hound Dog" is a sample of capitalist music, it's not as cruddy as our cultural commissars say.

I REMEMBER ANOTHER CONFABULATION WITH THE old man in the apartment over the airplane hangar: "Pasternak's book, which I personally never read, mind you, pissed off Stalin, pissed off our culture commissars, pissed off our security organs, which is why it will be published in Russia over Stalin's dead body. But here's the thing: When Stalin's wife died—she didn't shoot herself with the German pistol her brother gave her as some malicious tongues rumored, by the way, the Kremlin doctors who signed her death certificate said she died of appendicitis, the newspapers reported the cause of death as appendicitis, all that happened long before you were born—when she died, Pasternak was the only one to publish a condolence that came from the heart as opposed to the lobe of the brain that sucks up to power. Something about him being as shaken as if he had been a member of Stalin's family." The old man laughed under his iodine breath. "I can tell you that Stalin, mourning his dead wife, was moved by what Pasternak wrote and scribbled on his CheKist file, *Leave the cloud dweller in peace*. But it will be a cold day in the burning fiery furnace we call purgatory before Pasternak is invited to a family dinner at Stalin's table."

Maybe it was that same night or another night, I get confused about the order in which things happened, that the old man squatted in front of the parrot and began feeding him tiny bits of dried meat. I'd given him a present, one of the meerschaums my dad brought back from Cambridge, Britain, the time he attended a colloquium on Nernst's heat theorem which, being my father's son, I understand. I remember Koba couldn't stop thanking me, he was obviously not used to people turning up with presents. I could be wrong but I think there might have been a tear or two clouding his eyes as he examined the pipe. "You remind me of me when I was your age," I remember him telling me. "I addressed everyone—the teachers in the Gori elementary school, the director, the priests in the seminary, my father, even—using the familiar *ti*. Half the time they laughed. Half the time they slapped my face for being impertinent. You understand the word *impertinent*, kid?"

I didn't but, given what he said, I made an educated guess. "*Impertinent* is when someone my age speaks to someone your age using the familiar *ti*. Should I not have?"

Koba waved his crippled fingers at me. "In the old days everyone addressed the tsar with the formal *vui*. Only Grigori Rasputin, the sex-starved *starets* from the Tobolsk District, spoke to him man-to-man, using, without being invited, mind you, the informal *ti*. Which is how Rasputin, whose soul is surely roasting in the burning fiery furnace, wound up as the confessor to the tsar's wife. Ha! At the time of Rasputin's murder, tongues wagged—some people, me among them, thought he wound up warming the tsarina's bed. Which I suppose is why the individuals who killed him were said to have cut off his dick. *Sacré* Rasputin!"

I have this picture in my head of the old man trembling with laughter. I remember the laughter turning into a coughing fit. I remember the disgusting noise coming from the back of his throat when he coughed up phlegm into a large handkerchief. I watched him examining the phlegm as if it held secrets about the quantum field theory or the state of his health. A bit breathless, he asked, "How old are you, kid?"

"Twelve."

"You don't look twelve. You don't look a day more than nine. Ten at the most. You talk twelve but you look ten." The telephone on the desk rang. The old man glanced at it, then lifted it off its hook and set it back down again, cutting the connection without talking. "Fact of the matter is I don't like people. And people don't like me. Which is fine by me— wanting to be liked, *needing* to be liked, is a fatal handicap for anyone trying to help run a country. You inevitably wind up blaming someone else for whatever goes wrong—the peasants say a workman who fucks up will even blame his tools—and taking personal credit for everything that goes right. If we go an entire year without an airplane crash, if more men find work and factory production increases and fewer women die in childbirth, if our Russian explorers bobsled to the magnetic north pole, chalk it up to the popular leader who inspired them. Well, why not? That's as good an explanation as any for things going right." Koba stared off at a horizon that must have existed in his mind's eye. "You still here, kid? I forgot what I wanted to say. I forgot what we were talking about."

"You were talking about needing to be liked being a handicap."

"Needing to be liked is harder to kick than an opium habit. Feeling obliged to like the people around you is even harder. Hell, I try my damnedest to act as if I like Stalin's kittens and I fool them all, especially that Ukrainian fellow, Khrushchev, he thinks because I laugh at his dirty jokes I like the person who tells them."

A sopping wet smile trickled across Koba's jaw. I need to say on this occasion, on other occasions now that I think of it, his eyes had a different expression than his mouth, they were hard and angry, as if he was seeing himself in a coffin, while his mouth was soft and happy, as if he was, for the time of the smile, relieved to be alive. Which one was the real Koba, the eyes or the mouth? Hey, your guess is probably better than mine because I'm only a kid.

Like, there were things the old man said that I didn't hear because he was talking more to himself than to me. There were other things he said I heard but didn't understand. Still don't. I'll give you a for instance: "That American newspaperman," Koba mumbled, "his name was Steffens, Lincoln Steffens, he never said *I've seen the future and it works*. What he wrote in that telegram of his was *I've seen the future and it needs work*. But our expurgators edited out the word *needs*. It turned this Steffens fellow into a living legend."

FOUR

WHERE ISABEAU KEEPS BEATING THE KID AT HIS OWN GAME

FROM LEON'S NOTEBOOK:

ME: Like, did you ever see an actual execution?

THE OLD MAN: As a matter of fact I did, once, yes. In Tiflis, back in 1905. There was this vicious governor general of the Caucasus, name of Gryaznov, his Cossacks were rounding up revolutionists by the lorry-full, some of them were tortured to death, others were rotting in Gryaznov's citadel. The local Bolshevik cell—at twenty-eight I was the oldest member and the cell leader—voted to put an end to his reign of terror. We placed scraps of paper in a hat and drew lots to see who would have the honor of killing Gryaznov. The scrap with the X on it wound up in the hand of one of my best friends, a Georgian named Jorjiashvili. As he was quite inexperienced in what the Party called *wet work*, I decided to accompany him. Dressed in grease-stained tramway coveralls, carrying grenades hidden in leather pails, we made our way down Bariatinskaya Street to Alexander Park in front of the Governor's Palace. When the prick Gryaznov came out for his morning constitutional, Jorjiashvili and I pitched four grenades under his feet. The explosions rocked the park and filled it with smoke. Through the smoke I could see Gryaznov's Cossacks, their sabres flashing, galloping toward us. Jorjiashvili, the poor sapskull, lost his nerve and ran. The fucking Cossacks grabbed him as he tried to scamper over a wall. Shaking my head in feigned horror, I mingled with the crowd that had gathered around Gryaznov's mangled body. My young friend was sentenced to death before the sun set. That night carpenters erected a gallows in the great square of Tiflis. The next morning, with a mob of people looking on sullenly, the Cossacks dragged Jorjiashvili, whose ankles were chained so tightly he couldn't walk, up the wooden steps, fitted the thick rope around his neck and hanged him. Seeing the hanged man dancing on the end of the rope, a kind-hearted Orthodox priest grabbed hold of Jorjiashvili's bare feet and hung from them to put him out of his misery.

ME (*repeating the Russian proverb my dad would come up with when I complained about the teacher not understanding the subject she was teaching as well as I did*): Life is not a stroll across a field.

THE OLD MAN (*impatiently*): When we've constructed Communism in one country—in *this* country!—life will *become* a stroll across a field. That was the whole point of Jorjiashvili's sacrifice, it's the whole point of the sacrifices Stalin is obliged to demand of our people now. Do you understand what I'm saying or does it go in one ear and out the other?

ME: You're saying we need to be utopians before we catch sight of Utopia.

THE OLD MAN: How old did you say you were?

"ONE, TWO, THREE: *STONE!*"

"*Paper!* I win. Paper covers stone."

"One, two, three: *Paper!*"

"*Scissor!* Me again. Scissor cuts paper."

"One, two, three: *Scissor!*"

"*Stone!* Chalk up another win for female-ism. Stone crushes scissor."

"Hey, are you cheating, Isabeau?"

"How can you cheat at *scissor, stone, paper*, for gosh sake?"

"Well, it's creepy how you win all the time."

"I win all the time because I'm smarter than you," I told him.

And I am. Smarter than Leon. Smart enough to know when he raises one eyebrow, chances are good he's going to come out with the last thing I came out with. Smart enough to know his story of chit-chatting up an old man with iodine breath above an airplane hangar is pure fairy tale. Two scoops of vanilla ice cream covered in chocolate sauce, you wish! Smart enough to understand where the fairy tale comes from and spell it out for him—what with his father being dead and all, he's in the market for another father, even if he's not flesh and bones but a figment of his ten-year-old imagination.

"My imagination, like me, is ten and a half," he corrected me when I made the mistake of attributing the fairy tale to his ten-year-old imagination.

Me, too, I'm scared stiff. Me, too, I'm in the market for another father. What will become of us all, the twins Vladimir and Pavel, their half sister, Zinaida, Leon and me?

"You're making things up," I told him. "I don't believe a word about a secret door, a ballroom the size of an airplane hangar, the old man with the parrot—"

"Come with me next time—you'll see him for yourself."

"No way will you get me into that tunnel. I'll stick with the House on the Embankment and our secret rooms until my mother comes back from jail. Then we'll migrate to Uzbekistan and get out of Stalin's sight. Out of sight will, with any luck, be out of mind."

"I give you my word of honor, I'm telling you the truth," he said.

"I believe him," Vlad said.

"Me also, I believe him," Zinaida said.

"Thank you for that," Leon said.

Later, we were all sprawled on the floor of my secret room, Pavel and Vladimir (who we called Vlad), their older half sister Zinaida, Leon and me, playing Monopoly on the board the twins brought home from Washington, America, when their father, the deputy ambassador, was summoned back to Moscow and then shot as a CIA spy. On a small shortwave radio with a whopping antenna, the Voice of America was broadcasting jazz music by a guy named Dizzy something. "Frankly, I'm not impressed with capitalist music," I said, rolling the dice, then moving my tractor past

Go and collecting two hundred American dollars. "Our lives are complicated enough without you making up fairy tales about some old man living in a palace big enough to park two giant bomber planes." I threaded my fingers through Leon's wild hair. He loves when I do this. When he's excited, which is most of the time, it calms him down. "Guards playing chess, rifles stacked against the wall, a housekeeper named Valechka. What will you invent next?"

"Next," Leon told me, "I'll invent our mothers being released from jail." The words came out of his mouth with tears in his voice, which made me want to cry too. I slung one arm over his shoulder and gave him a squeeze.

It helped. A little. Well, not much. "Our mothers haven't committed a crime," I said in a whisper. "When the authorities realize this they will trip over their own feet apologizing for having arrested them and drive them home in one of those shiny black cars of theirs. And our families"—now it was my voice that had tears in it—"our families, minus our fathers, will go back to living as we always lived."

Pavel, still trying to get out of the Monopoly prison, was trying to impress me by smoking one of those hollow-tipped Kazbek Papirosi, the only problem being he'd turned green. With the cigarette glued to his wobbly lip, he threw the dice in the hope of rolling doubles. "Does this old man of yours have any kids?" he asked. Leon appreciated the question because it meant Pavel, unlike me, believed his fairy tale.

"Two sons that he knows about, one died during the war in a German prisoner-of-war camp. Also a daughter who he said is married to someone he's not all that hot about."

"How could Leon know all this if he wasn't telling the truth?" Vlad asked me.

Leon looked straight at me when he replied to Vlad. "I know all this because the old man told me."

Leon stuck to his fairy tale. "Have you got any children?" he remembered asking the old man the third time he claimed to have climbed the spiral staircase to the apartment over the colossal ballroom.

"What makes you ask?" the old man replied, if you believe Leon.

Leon said he told him, "You can tell an awful lot about a grown-up by the way he deals with his kids. My friend Isabeau's dad treated her as a piece of furniture. My father taught me quantum physics and chess."

"My dad treated me as a piece of *expensive* furniture," I corrected him. "What did your fictional old man say then?"

"He told me he'd tried to learn how to play chess once," Leon said. "He told me it was when he was deported to Siberia because of his revolutionist activities."

"And you believed him? You swallowed the story about him being deported to Siberia?"

For sure, my friend Leon is going to be a novelist when he grows up. He kept adding details to his fictional story every time he told it. "You could see the old man was enjoying the confabulation with me," Leon said with a straight face. "He liked hearing himself talk, he liked recollecting things that happened to him when he was young. It was almost as if he was reliving the things that happened to him when he was young. He told me the tsarist police deported him to Siberia not once. Not twice. Seven times! He said he spent ten whole years in Siberian jails, if you can call a peasant's shack a jail. Six of those times he escaped, sometimes after being there for only a month or two. When a political reached Siberia, according to him the warder would ask whether you planned to escape immediately or wait until the spring thaw. You can't make up details like that. He said the tsarist police could never pin the bank robberies or elimination of enemies on him, so they wound up charging him with distributing pamphlets or organizing May Day parades or running an illegal printing press. He claimed the Cossack guards, who harassed other politicals, kept their distance from him—they thought, what with him being part Ossetian, he could press two fingers on their throats, Caucasian style, and cut off the oxygen in their windpipes. The last time he was deported his sentence was cut short, it was in 1917, when mobs of women took to the streets of Petrograd to demand bread. It was the women who made the revolution, he told me, it was the women who forced the tsar to abdicate. 'The peasants have a saying,' he told me. 'Little sparks light great fires.' Hey, you understand the word *abdicate*, Isabeau?"

"I'm not stupid, stupid. I know the story. It's when the tsar stopped being tsar. First he lost his job. Then he lost his head."

" 'I was in the village of Kureika in the Turakhansk Government beyond the Arctic Circle,' " Leon—sticking to his fairy tale, reading from notes he'd scribbled in his lined notebook—quoted the old man saying, " 'when word reached us of what had happened in Petrograd. I woke up one morning to find the guards had melted away. The local police station, if you can call a one-room hut with mud walls and a thatched roof a police station, was deserted. The convicts' files had been burned in the potbellied stove. I packed my gear and walked two hundred kilometers across the frozen taiga to the nearest town, and got on the first train heading west, and wound up in Petrograd working with Comrade Stalin, who—until Lenin returned from European exile—was the senior Bolshevik there at the time.' "

"What was Petrograd like when he got there?"

" 'In a word, Petrograd was a madhouse. I thought the Provisional Government had let all the lunatics out of the asylums. Soldiers and sailors and workers raced through the streets flaunting banners and shouting slogans that challenged the banners and slogans of the Mensheviks and Social Revolutionaries racing through the same streets in the other direction. The Provisional Government issued orders that nobody obeyed. The Grand Duke Nicholas Nikolaevich was reappointed commander in chief of Russia's eleven-million-man army, only to be fired hours later. Exiles were flooding back into the city, rents doubled overnight, inflation soared, food became scarce. There was no garbage collection because there was no garbage—everything got eaten. Wounded soldiers with boxes of hard-to-find Army-issue matches stood on street corners and for a kopek or two would light your cigarette for you. That little shit Alexander Kerensky, the Provisional Government's minister of war before he became the Provisional Government's prime minister, moved into the tsar's bedroom in the Winter Palace. Stalin and I set up shop in a little room on Basseinaya Street, working out of there we took over *Pravda* and began the tedious task of organizing the Bolshevik cadres for the revolution Lenin said was inevitable. You're thinking—ha! I can see the smoke coming out your ears—if revolution was so fucking inevitable why did we have to bother organizing the Bolshevik cadres? The answer is, it was Stalin's organizing the Bolshevik cadres that made Lenin's revolution inevitable. Listen, the absolute power the tsar had abandoned festered in the gutters of Petrograd. The burning question was who would have the mettle to pick it up.' "

LEON, WHO WAS THE HOUSE'S RESIDENT CHESS master, read us part of another confabulation he claimed to have had with the old man. "Did you ever learn to play chess during your years in Siberia?" he claims to have asked this Koba person.

If you believe Leon, which I'm not sure I do, the old man laughed or cleared his throat, apparently it was sometimes impossible to tell which. " 'I could never get it straight how the pieces moved,' " he is supposed to have told Leon. " 'Some of them could jump over the pawns, others you had to move the pawn out of the way to clear a path for them. Maybe you could teach me sometime.' "

"The way the pieces move is the easiest part," Leon says he said. "My dad always claimed you need to be paranoid to be a good chess player. You need to seriously believe your opponent is out to murder your queen and emasculate your king. Hey, Koba, knowing you I'll bet you understand *emasculate*. A good chess player knows the word *opponent* is too polite. The other guy's not your *opponent*, he's your *arch-enemy*. You can bet a hidden threat lurks behind every move he makes—pawn to king five may look innocent enough at first glance, but five or ten moves down the road it will bite you."

" 'What you're saying interests me, kid. You could make the case I played the kind of chess you're describing when I advised Stalin on how to deal with American President Roosevelt and British First Minister Churchill at Teheran in '43. I told him to assume every word they uttered, every document they asked him to sign, every seemingly innocent offer they put on the table contained a hidden threat, a capitalist land mine that was going to explode under his feet if he didn't watch his step.' " Leon swears he heard the old man chuckling to himself. Leon wanted me to believe he asked the old man why he was chuckling to himself. " 'The state banquets were pure torture,' " Leon remembered the old man remembering. " 'There was one waitperson posted behind every guest. There were two bearded Chechens in monkey suits who did nothing but pour wine. There was a Negro busboy who replaced your ashtray seconds after you stubbed out a cigarette in it. There was a hotchpotch of forks and knives and spoons, there were wineglasses and vodka glasses and champagne glasses and water glasses and cognac glasses. I'd skipped lunch that day—I had put on weight and decided to diet—and was dying of hunger but I couldn't begin eating until Roosevelt or Churchill began eating so I wouldn't make a fool of myself using the wrong fork or knife or spoon. Back in the Caucasus, men open their pocketknives and set them next to the plate, when they use plates, and eat with their fingers. Want to treat yourself to a good laugh, kid, imagine the look on American President

Roosevelt's patrician face if I had cut the meat with my pocketknife and started eating with my fingers.'"

"Hey, did esteemed Comrade Stalin take your advice about the capitalist land mine?" Leon says he asked.

"'Whether or not he took my advice is a state secret. As you're only a kid, you're not cleared for state secrets. I could tell you but then I'd have to kill you.'"

"You're, like, kidding, right?"

"'If you think so.'"

Fact is, Leon wasn't positive the old man was kidding and, if you can swallow his story, he decided he didn't want to know if the old man was kidding. "I'm particularly interested in Siberia these days," Leon, hoping to change the subject, swears he told his fictional old man. "I've never met anybody who's been there. So, hey, what was it like?"

He read out the alleged old man's supposed answer from his lined notebook. "'In a word, it was so cold your eyelids could freeze closed if you fell asleep outside. I spent most of my time cutting firewood and feeding the stove in the peasant's hut I shared with two other politicals. Luckily for us the peasant was a fisherman. He fished the river when it wasn't frozen over, he fished the sea when it was. He kept us alive, though you have to like fish to eat it for breakfast and supper seven days a week. When a prisoner died we fought over his books. I usually won. Once I finished reading them I used the pages to light the fire in the stove. We scored vodka when the boat came upriver every six months but it was so cold even the vodka froze—the only way to drink it was to suck on vodka icicles. If you pissed outside, the piss would freeze before it hit the ground. At night I would light the little tallow lamp and read Lenin aloud to the fishermen. I tried to persuade them to join the Bolshevik crusade, but it turned out to be impossible to explain the dictatorship of the proletariat to illiterate peasants who worshipped the water god Teb-Tengri.'"

"You got to be exaggerating," Leon supposedly told the old man, but I hung on to these stories about Siberia even if they were a figment of Leon's imagination. Just the word Siberia caused tears to well up in my eyes. "Our moms are probably in Siberia," I remarked by way of explaining the tears. "My mom was arrested in the clothes she had on her back. She'll freeze to death in Siberia."

It was true for Leon's mom also. He remembered watching her arrest through the crack in the plaster. He remembered her putting on her warmest winter coat. But she hadn't been wearing her thick woollen stockings and fur-lined winter boots, she'd been wearing the flat-soled white shoes she wore when she had the night shift in the Kremlin hospital.

Suddenly I was sorry I'd egged Leon on about Siberia.

After a time us kids got bored playing Monopoly and decided to explore the gigantic vaulted basements in the House on the Embankment. Pavel produced one of those giant shears that can cut through chains and padlocks in case we came across chains or padlocks. "Where'd you get that?" I asked.

"My uncle Fyodor used it to steal bicycles locked to fences behind gymnasiums," he explained. "After he was arrested for selling counterfeit ration coupons we all got to take things from his room in the communal apartment.

My mom took his desk chair, my aunt Elizaveta took his not-counterfeit ration cards and a photo album, I took this. A kid never knows when he's going to need to break a padlock, huh?"

The bunch of us scrambled down the stairwells to the minus-two level and ran through the dimly lit passageways to the basketball court. The door was fastened with a padlock so thick we couldn't cut through it, even with two of us pushing on each handle of the giant scissors.

"Let's try the pool," Zinaida whispered and we raced off, giggling, down another passageway to the double door. You could smell the chlorine seeping under the closed doors. The padlock was thinner and with two of us pushing on each handle of the cutter we managed to snap it off. The broken lock clattered onto the stone floor. The twins cheered as the five of us pushed through the doors. The pool, which was advertised as being Olympic-sized, whatever that meant, was dimly lit by the red exit lights over the doors and the red dressing rooms sign at the other end, but your eyes quickly became used to the darkness. The twins stripped to the skin and plunged in. "It's warm as a bathtub," Vlad called, his voice echoing across the surface of the water. Zinaida, who was the oldest of our bunch, stripped down to her underwear—she actually wore one of her mother's brassieres stuffed with cotton because she's almost fifteen and mortified not to have bigger boobs. I went off to a bench on the side and, thinking the dimness would be murky enough to mask me, took off my clothes, all of them, every stitch. This was, to use one of Leon's expressions, a major event in my life. I'd never been stark naked in the presence of kids my own age before. In front of kids any age before. Which probably explained why I was holding my breath. Which probably explained the cramp in the pit of my stomach. When I turned and stepped onto the diving board, I spotted Leon gawking at me across the pool. As I could see the tiny nipples on my tiny breasts (hey, I'm only eleven and a bit) I guessed he could too. I could make out that Leon, like me, he had no hair down there, you know, in the crotch region. And I suddenly twigged to what he was staring at—the emptiness, the absence in the female crotch. What did he expect? In his defense, he probably didn't know enough to know what to expect. What he needed was a father to explain the weak nuclear force and female anatomy to him. What he didn't have was a father to explain anything to him. Another emptiness, another absence. If there really was an old man living above a giant airplane hangar at the Moscow end of the tunnel, which, given Leon's loose relationship with the truth, I very much doubted, maybe he could get him to explain this particular fact of life.

Now that I think of it, this was the first time I toyed with the idea Leon's fairy tale might not be a fairy tale.

"So admit it," I shouted to Leon across the pool, logging my voice with laughter to cover my discomfiture, "you've never seen a girl without clothes before, right?" I was delighting in his discomfiture. I imagined him blushing like a bowl of borscht as he carefully backed down the ladder into the pool. I climbed to the tippy tip of the diving board and jack-knifed into the darkness. Underwater the silence whelmed me. The water was every bit as warm as a bathtub. When I came up for air the vapor rising off the surface made it feel as if we were swimming in a thick fog, thank goodness for small favors. Zinaida was the only one who really knew how to swim—her mother had once been on the Soviet women's swim team, which probably explained why. The apple never falls far . . . The rest of us just flapped around until our skin wrinkled.

"SO YOU ACTUALLY ASKED THIS OLD MAN OF YOURS?"

Leon, who was never able to hide anything from me, nodded grudgingly.

"Okay, let's say, for argument's sake, he exists. What did he say?"

"He said he was all ears."

"What the hell did that mean?"

"It meant, like, the subject under discussion interested him. He was puffing away on one of those foul-smelling Herzegovina Flors that my father loved and my mother loathed. 'Exactly what did you see when you went to swim in the compound pool?' he demanded. I could see him leaning over his desk, the cigarette bobbling on his lower lip, hanging on my every word. I could see beads of sweat on his forehead. The blotches on his scalp glowed—but maybe I was, like, imagining this detail. When the ash grew long on his cigarette, I pointed at it with my chin and the old man flicked the ash into the artillery shell he used as an ashtray. 'Answer,' he said impatiently, so I answered. I described how you stripped to the skin. I described, no offense intended, your absent breasts. When I came to your crotch I think I might have stammered. 'Spit it out!' the old man ordered in a tone that made me suspect he was accustomed to giving orders. And I did. I worked up my nerve and I spit it out—I described the gash in your crotch that seemed to me to be a wound. The old man stopped me right there. 'What you were looking at, kid, is the origin of the universe. What you were looking at is where civilization begins.' To tell you the god-awful truth, Isabeau, I wasn't sure I understood. 'The universe begins in Isabeau's crotch?' I repeated. My bewilderment obviously tickled the old man."

"'*The universe begins in the female crotch?*' Holy gorillas, I'm beginning to believe you, Leon. You're incapable of making up something like that."

"I tried to put the confabulation on safer ground by pleading innocence," Leon went on. "'Like, I'm not really twelve years old,' I admitted to him. "'I'm only ten and a half.'"

"What did your fictional old man say to that?"

"My factual old man said something along the lines of 'If you count dog years, me too, I'm ten and a half.' Which only added to my bewilderment, Isabeau. What are dog years? And how can an old man be ten and a half? He looked old enough to be dead."

FIVE

WHERE THE KID ADMITS TO HAVING BITTEN THE BULLET

FROM LEON'S NOTEBOOK:

THE OLD MAN: Listen, kid, poetry, prose, art, architecture, theatre scripts, screenplays, history, especially history—everything must be at the beck and call of the Revolution, of the Party.

ME: How can history be at the beck and call of anything except historical fact?

THE OLD MAN (*laughing under his iodine breath*): Written history tells us more about the historian than history. It tells us what the historian has decided to remember. The Party can help him decide what to remember.

ME: Is there anything beyond the beck and call of the Party?

THE OLD MAN: The gravedigger and the grave he digs is beyond the beck and call of the Party.

ME AGAIN. LEON SPEAKING. NOT SURE ISABEAU
got all the details straight—it's within the realm of
probability that I didn't tell her the juiciest parts of my
confabulation with the old man. When he said something
about the origins of the universe being in the female crotch,
I can say now, though I couldn't work up the nerve to say
to Isabeau, that the kopek dropped. I remember asking the
old man, "Is it or isn't it the cunt thing you talked about?"
At which point he began choking on laughter that seemed
to originate in his belly. Through the cloud of cigarette
smoke I could make out one of those twisted smiles on his
lips—I say *twisted* because it really looked as if trying to
smile caused him physical pain, like when you accidentally
hit your elbow against a sink. And, oh boy, were his teeth
stained brown from the cigarettes.

When he could finally speak, he said something along
the lines of: "You're not as dumb as you look, kid."

He pulled open a drawer of his desk and tossed me
another packet of rubles bound in a rubber band. Then he
got up and went over to his parrot and, opening the little
bamboo door, reached in and took the bird out of the cage.
He held it up to his face and looked it in the eye. "What are
you going to—" I started to say but I never got to finish my
sentence. I knew what he was going to do before he did it.
He twisted the bird's hooked beak in one direction and its
body in another direction.

Thinking I might throw up, I jerked my head to one
side. "Why?" I whispered.

"Parrots are not innocent," is what I remember him
saying. Then he did something I hadn't seen before—he

smiled an ordinary, everyday smile, the way my dad used to smile when he heard me explaining the quantum field model of the weak nuclear force to my mom, which is to say with his eyes and his mouth on the same page. Obviously tickled with himself, the old man added a postscriptum: "Listen up, kid. Hang on my every word. What I'm going to tell you comes straight from the horse's mouth. *Nobody is innocent!*"

"Identify the horse's mouth."

"Dumb question for a smart-ass kid like you. In the Soviet Union there is only one horse's mouth—his given name happens to be the same as mine, Joseph, and his surname is Stalin."

"And esteemed Comrade Stalin really thinks nobody's innocent? Even members of the politburo?"

"Ha! That's rich. *Especially* members of the politburo."

WHEN I REACHED THE OLD MAN'S APARTMENT THE day before, I found him propped up on pillows in his enormous bed. "Come on in, damn it," he called when he saw me hesitate at the doorway. "Where the hell have you been? You were supposed to be here twenty minutes ago."

I spotted twelve or fifteen medals pinned on his tunic where there had been none before. "Wow," I remember saying, "you *are* a war hero."

The old man nodded toward a shoebox filled with medals open on the night table. "There are a lot more where these came from. I don't have room for them all on my tunic. I thought you'd get a kick out of seeing me with my medals on."

"My father had four medals," I told him, "not counting the one he got posthumously after the chain reaction
killed him."

The old man cleared his throat, which meant he was
about to make an important announcement. "I like having
you around, kid," is what he said. "You bring out the best
in me. I'm beginning to think of you as a surrogate son. I
don't lose sleep worrying you want to take my place helping
Stalin run the country, which is more than can be said for
some of his precious kittens who would be only too happy
to see me stumble. Fact is, I do stumble now and then—who
doesn't?—but, as the peasants say, a stumble can prevent a
fall." I have this picture in my brain of Koba leaning forward
and reaching behind himself to fluff up the pillows, then
carefully sinking back into them. "Stalin liked having Sergei
Kirov around," he went on, dredging up something from
the past that Koba the historian had chosen to remember.
"He treated him like a goddamn surrogate son. He told
people Kirov brought out the best in him. They had a father-
surrogate-son relationship, or so Stalin thought. He spent
long evenings in the sauna with him drinking vodka and
solving the world's problems, for Christ's sake. And how
did the shit repay him?"

I didn't know how this Kirov guy repaid esteemed Comrade Stalin and admitted as much to Koba.

Suddenly the old man, breathing heavily through his
nostrils, was seething. "He repaid him by upstaging him at
the Party Congress. *Upstaging Joseph Stalin!* Kirov delivered
a stem-winder of a speech—speaking in fucking flawless
Russian, articulating each word without a trace of Stalin's

Georgian accent, he fed red meat to the Party carnivores, attacking oppositionists who weren't at the beck and call of the Party. The *apparatchiks* in the hall went wild, they were whistling, they were clapping their sweaty hands, they were stamping their feet, they were chanting *Lock 'em up, lock 'em up*. Which is how Stalin, who was able to read the tea leaves where others just drank the tea, understood the prick of a mayor from Leningrad was out to take his place. Well, we all know how that ended."

"I don't know. How did it end?"

"It ended with some lunatic shooting Kirov in the goddamn neck. It goes without saying, rumors that the assassin—who, mind you, confessed to his crime before his execution—was somehow connected to our CheKists were pure unadulterated slander. In public, Stalin organized a state funeral for Kirov and led the country in mourning his late but certainly not lamented surrogate son. In private, he was heard to say, *Good riddance to stinking rubbish*."

THE NEXT TIME I CLIMBED THE SPIRAL STEEL stairs to his Little Corner apartment, which, according to my notebook, was two-slant-three-hundred-sixty-fifths of a year later, the bamboo birdcage was gone and the old man was sitting on the floor, his back to the tiled stove, a half-empty vodka bottle and a half-empty glass next to him, looking at photographs in an album. "I hear they have invented film that takes pictures in color," he muttered. I had to strain to catch what he was saying because he was, as often happened, talking to himself. "Personally I prefer black and white." Looking up, he discovered I was in the room. "You here?

Here, take a look at this, kid. These snapshots date back to before the Revolution. You'll see what I looked like when I still had a full head of hair." He pointed to a photograph of a lady—she was wearing what looked like a thin summer frock and staring defiantly, her eyes open wide and probably not blinking, her head tilted, straight into the camera. "On second thought color photos might be better after all," the old man said. "Her eyes were green."

"Who is she?"

"Her name was Nadezhda. She was one of those Bolshevik intellectuals who could recite entire passages from Lenin's *What Is To Be Done?* She knew Lenin personally but unlike me she actually admired him. It's possible that had something to do with his not being indifferent to girls who didn't wear rigid undergarments. Krupskaya, his bitch of a wife, wore a medieval breastplate under her blouse, so we joked. His French girlfriend, Inessa, like my Tatka, didn't hide her ladylikeness under undergarments. Listen, one of the great things about revolution is that female revolutionists are passionate about liberating their bodies as well as their minds. Sexually speaking, our Bolshevik Revolution was a field day for male revolutionists like me willing to help them liberate their bodies. That's something else they don't teach in the schools. Here, this one is a photograph I took of Lenin before the Revolution. When the Provisional Government put a price on his head and he had to go into hiding, he lived for a time in Nadezhda's parents' apartment in Petrograd. That's the great man himself sitting on the daybed next to Nadezhda. She refused to wash her hand for a week the first time Lenin shook it. She was one of the few people who could decipher his indecipherable handwriting and wound up typing his letters and the articles he wrote for *Pravda*. She told me Lenin couldn't spell to save his life. She corrected what he wrote as she typed." He flipped to another page filled with snapshots of this Nadezhda lady. "Her parents didn't appreciate it when I courted her. She was still a teenager at the time, they decided there was too much difference in our ages."

"Was she your wife?" I asked, but he seemed lost in his remembrances and didn't answer.

"It's true she was younger than me," he finally said, scratching absently at his scalp, shaking his head in what I took to be bittersweetness. "Twenty-two years younger, to be exact, but she talked old. There were times . . . times when she talked too old. Like when she repeated these cock-and-bull stories of starving children with swollen stomachs begging at train stations in the Ukraine, as if I was responsible for the famine when anyone could see it was the fault of the fucking peasants who burned their crops and killed their cows rather than join the fucking collective. And then that son of a bitch of a brother of hers came back from Germany with a present for her. He couldn't bring her a necklace or a bracelet, oh no, not him, he had to bring her a pistol, for Christ's sake." The old man caught his breath. "The real difference between my Tatka and me wasn't our ages," he muttered. "It was the way we looked at the world. It was our eyes. Hers were seaweed green. Mine are like Ivan the Dread's—coal black."

Staring off into a private long-ago only he could see, words came spilling through his lips so fast they tripped over each other. Here, to the best of my recollection, is the nitty-gritty of what he said: "Nadezhda became exasperated with me. I don't deny I may have now and then flirted with the ladies at state banquets, what Georgian in the prime of life doesn't play the field, but my Tatka had a lot in common with the dark side of the moon, she could be moody as hell, she would hold grudges for weeks when we quarrelled, which was frequently. In one of her black moods she packed her bags and left me, I remember the year, I remember the hour, it was eleven in the morning in 1926, she ran off to Petrograd with our children. Like some lovesick idiot I went racing after her, I played the role fate assigned to me, I begged her to come back. She finally agreed on condition we would never sleep in the same bed again."

"Hey, Koba, I'm not stupid," I remember telling the old man. "I see what you're saying—she agreed to return on condition there would be no more sexual intercourse."

The old man came back from the long-ago and focused on the here and now, with me in the foreground. "You remind me of my Nadezhda, kid—you also talk old. Watch out, it can land you up shit creek."

Though there seemed to be a couple of spare bedrooms in the apartment, I hadn't seen any lady around other than the housekeeper, Valechka. "Where is Nadezhda now?" I asked.

"Rotting in some fucking cemetery."

I murmured the sentence my parents taught me to say in situations like this: "I'm sorry for your loss."

"Listen, kid, the last thing I need is your goddamn sympathy," the old man growled angrily. His anger left me tongue-tied. It left him tongue-tied too. After a bit he untied his tongue. "I'm tired," he announced, very quietly. Too quietly. "You should probably go home now." He was still turning the pages of his photo album when I tiptoed out.

SO I SUPPOSE, AT SOME POINT, I NEED TO TELL YOU about the dead man.

Pavel and Vlad and me, we were in Pavel and Vlad's secret room, which was diagonally across and further down the secret passageway from my room, playing a game I invented called Yloponom, which is Monopoly spelled backward. I came up with the idea of playing the game backward to make it more Communistical. In my version, the players start off owning all the properties and try to lose their hotels and their houses and their money and finally the properties themselves by landing on someone else's property and paying rent. I even made up little penalty cards, like where you had to bribe the NKVD *earphone*, our slang for *stool pigeon*, two hundred US dollars to not report you for listening to the Voice of America, that kind of thing. The first player to go bankrupt is declared the perfect proletarian and the winner. Having run out of cash, I was about to mortgage Boardwalk when I heard what sounded like a scuffle in the passageway. Pavel and I exchanged scared looks. Then we heard the shrill voice of Isabeau crying out, "You're hurting me!" A moment later the door flew open and Isabeau came tumbling in, followed, boy oh boy, by a big man wearing one of those ankle-long raincoats even though it wasn't raining out. "You kids have got to stop eating in the canteen downstairs if you want to hide in the House on the Embankment," is what he said. He was swallowing a laugh as he plopped himself down on Pavel's cot. "You also need to make your bed while your mother's away," he said, ironing Pavel's rumpled sheets with the flat of his palm. There was an ugly smirk planted on his ugly lips. "Where did you get the rubles to pay the cashier?" he demanded, looking from Pavel to me to Vlad to Isabeau to Zinaida, in the corner reading one of her American Batman comics. When nobody answered, he swallowed another laugh. "Cat got your tongue?" he asked, looking straight at me.

It was Vlad, normally more timid than the rest of us combined, who managed to locate his vocal cords. "What do you want from us?"

"That depends on what you have?"

Zinaida brought the open comic book up to cover her chest so the man in the raincoat wouldn't think she had breasts just because she wore one of her mother's brassieres.

"He was waiting for me in our apartment," Isabeau told us, fighting back tears. "He twisted my arm behind my back when I wouldn't answer his questions. So I answered his questions."

The man produced one of those silver lighters with esteemed Comrade Stalin's profile on it and, tilting his head, carefully aimed the tiny flamethrower at the end of the cigarette between his lips. "Can I offer any of you kids a cigarette? No? Don't tell me you don't smoke yet. At your age I was doing half a pack a day. Just as well you don't smoke. There are doctors who believe smoking isn't good for your lungs.

On my list of threats to my life, smoking is right down near the basement. So I figured it out," he said, exhaling a perfect smoke ring, then breaking it with the flat of his hand so he could see us better. "You're all the children of enemies of the people who have been arrested. If your parents lived in the House on the Embankment, it means they had cash, and plenty of it, which is how come you kids have rubles to pay the cashier in the canteen."

Vlad—did I, like, change my opinion of him that day!—repeated his question. "What is it you want?"

"Money. Thick packets of it. Otherwise I'll come back with my pals and arrest the lot of you for trespassing in apartments the NKVD has put off-limits. You did see the duct tape across the front doors? There are special camps in our gulag for children of anti-Soviet elements."

I finally managed to find my voice. "How much money?"

"For starters, let's say a thousand rubles each."

"Where would we find five thousand rubles!" Zinaida burst out.

"I can see you're good at arithmetic," the man said with a lecherous grin. He was staring at the comic book covering her chest. "If you want to keep on living here, you kids need to come up with the cash. Your parents, like all *apparatchiks*, will have stashed wads of rubles away against a rainy day." He pulled the collar of his raincoat up around his bull's neck. "In a manner of speaking, it's raining out today even though it's not raining out today."

"If we were to s-s-somehow find five thousand r-r-rubles," I said, "how d-d-do we know you won't come b-b-back for more?" It was only after I posed the question that I realized I was stammering.

"You c-c-can't know," he said, mimicking me. "B-b-but I don't see where you have m-m-much of a choice." He stood up and craned his head from side to side as if he was working out a crinkle in his neck. "I'll be back tomorrow, count on it. Okay? Look, it's okay if it's not okay but I advise you kids to think hard about the long train ride to Siberia. You'll be en route for weeks, maybe even months. And the cattle cars don't come equipped with flush toilets, not to mention a canteen like the one here in the House on the Embankment."

"I'm frightened," Pavel said when the man in the raincoat had gone.

"What are we going to do?" Zinaida asked plaintively.

"We could report him to the police," Vlad offered.

"He is the police," I said.

"We could pay him with Monopoly money," Zinaida said. "If he's never been to America he might not know the difference."

"We need to be careful not to get him angry," Isabeau said. "I got him angry. My arm still hurts."

"Maybe we ought to leave the House before he comes back," Vlad said.

"Where would we go?" Zinaida asked. "Who would take us in?"

"If we're not here, how will we know when our mothers come back?" Isabeau said.

I have this picture in my brain of the five of us sitting on the floor, our backs against the wall, hoping against hope one of us would come up with a solution.

That *one of us* turned out to be me. After an eternity I was flabbergasted to hear myself tell the others, "Like, I think I know what we need to do."

"WHAT'S YOUR FAVORITE THING TO DO?" I REMEMber asking the old man.

He hadn't shaved in days. The stubble of a beard the color of sidewalk had turned his skin into sandpaper. He thought for a moment. "Nowadays I like to watch parades. As I help run the country I get to watch the big Red Square parades from the top of Lenin's tomb. It's a great place to stand. The floorboards are heated in winter. All those factory workers and soldiers parading through Red Square are freezing their balls off. But up on the reviewing stand our feet are snug as bugs in a bearskin rug. And there's a table behind us filled with *zakouski* and hot Georgian wine in thermos bottles."

"That's where esteemed Comrade Stalin stands!" I heard myself say.

"I especially like military parades," the old man was still talking, though once again he was his own audience. "I get a kick out of watching the goliath tanks and those phallic rockets and the perfect rows of soldiers in lockstep pass the reviewing stand. If someone is out of step I count the rows back from the front and the number in and report it to the general drinking warm wine from a thermos."

"My dad taught me that tattle-taling isn't nice. The poor soldier may have frozen feet but he'll be in hot water."

The old man realized I was still in the room. "His job in life is to walk in lockstep. All violations must be punished.

Failure to punish would be unfair to the others who make the effort to walk in lockstep."

"My mom used to laugh when she saw the soldiers walking in lockstep in the movies. She said men were not born to walk in lockstep."

The old man shrugged wearily. "Some are, some aren't. The job of an assistant tsar, like me, is to separate the two groups and then leapfrog to the front and lead those who have the good sense to walk in lockstep." A quirky glint appeared in the old man's watery eyes. "When I was young I didn't walk in lockstep," he admitted. "But times were different. If you walked in lockstep back then, you were parading for the tsar. Come to think of it, I did everything out of lockstep in those days. I specialized in what the Party in the Caucasus called *dry* work—shaking down rich merchants—and the occasional *wet* work—liquidating the ones who refused to be shaken down. To be honest, I enjoyed the life. You were outdoors most of the time. It was a lot of fun robbing armored wagons delivering cash to banks, it was a lot of fun fucking the girls who were attracted to Bolsheviks robbing armored wagons."

"Did you ever personally shoot somebody?"

The old man cleared his throat. "I may have."

"Did you kill the person you shot?"

"I was Lenin's brigand at the time. I didn't hang around to take the pulse of someone bleeding on the ground. If I shot at someone I shot to kill. As I was a damn good shot I didn't usually miss."

I think it was then that I understood I was in the presence of a Soviet celebrity, a genuine hero of our glorious

Revolution. Koba not only looked old but he smelled old—still, from that moment on I saw him with new eyes. I remember asking him if it had made him sad to kill somebody, even if the cause was a noble one. He didn't clear his throat. He answered straightaway. "Revolutionists," he informed me, "don't cry over spilt milk. Stalin teaches us that it's stupid to think the passage from capitalism to socialism can happen without violence. Listen, kid, the first order of business in life—for an individual, for the Revolution—is to survive, okay. And to survive you need to identify your enemies. Or as Stalin teaches us, identify those who risk to become enemies *before* they have a chance to become enemies, and then make it your business to eliminate them."

"What you're saying is I wouldn't get in trouble if I eliminated someone who was threatening the survival of me or my friends?"

A mule's bray escaped from the gorge of the old man's throat. "Don't get caught and you won't get in trouble," is what I remember him saying. I swear those were his exact words: Don't get caught. He sucked on his cigarette as if it was one of those oxygen masks I'd seen in my mother's ward of the Kremlin hospital. Then he added, "If someone is threatening you or your friends, eliminating him comes under the heading of self-defense."

"SELF-DEFENSE? YOU'RE SURE THAT'S WHAT YOUR old man said?" Isabeau asked. "Is he a lawyer or a judge?"

"He's an assistant tsar," I said. "He helps run the country."

"Not sure what that job description means exactly," Isabeau said.

"Maybe he shines Comrade Stalin's shoes," Zinaida said. "Maybe that's his idea of helping run the country."

"You don't understand," I said. "He's obviously a hero of the Revolution."

"Hero, schmero," Isabeau said. "What we need is someone who knows someone in the Kremlin who can get this NKVD dude off our backs."

Trouble was, we didn't know anybody who knew anybody in the Kremlin.

SO I NEED TO DO IT, I NEED TO BITE THE BULLET and tell you about when I bit the bullet. Here goes nothing: He came back, the Raincoat in the raincoat, like he said he would. Isabeau told him to follow her through the passageway to the landing inside the fire door that led to the wooden staircase. The rest of us were sitting on the steps going up, waiting for him. I nodded toward the brown paper bag on Zinaida's mom's Indian rug that we'd set out on the floor.

"What's with the rug?" Raincoat demanded.

"We didn't want you to dirty your knees when you counted the money," I said.

Raincoat smiled that nasty smile of his as he knelt down on the rug and opened the bag and pulled out the wad of rubles the old man had given me from his desk drawer stuffed with rubles. Then, wetting his thumb on his tongue, Raincoat snapped off the rubber band and began to count out the bills. The other kids looked at me, their eyes wide with an unasked question. I concentrated on the back of

Raincoat's neck as I took hold of my mother's Chagan that I'd wrapped in a towel the way I'd seen capitalist crooks do in the movies. I came up behind him as he said, "Who do you think you're fooling, huh? There's only two thousand four hundred—"

Those were his dying words. I reached out with my arm and pointed the towel at his thick neck and, boy oh boy, I squeezed the trigger, I really did, I squeezed one of the five bullets out of the towel smack into the guy's neck. There was a soft *pling* that was surprisingly comforting, don't ask me why, there was a wisp of smoke rising from the end of the rolled towel almost as if I'd shot him with my mom's towel and not my mom's pistol. I noticed this little hole in the back of his neck that hadn't been there before. It must have been about then Raincoat slumped forward, his forehead bumped onto the floor and he lay there perfectly balanced, his knees, his forehead, his two elbows touching the rug, a thin foam seeping from his dead lips.

Picture it—or, hey, don't if you're squeamish. Isabeau was sobbing quietly. "Think of it as self-defense," I whispered to her as the other four of us, one on each end of the rug, struggled Raincoat's body down the stairs. Vlad went ahead to hold open the doors. I could smell the chlorine from the pool before we reached the minus-two basement and sucked it in through my nostrils in the hope it would disinfect the odors sure to be coming from the dead man we were hauling to our improvised cemetery.

"I'M GOOD AT CHESS AND I WAS GOOD AT SCHOOL when I went to school," I remember telling the old man one night. "My father was good at physics. My mother is good at heart surgery. What are you especially good at?"

"Making boots. When I was your age I worked in my father's shop. I should say I worked in his shop when he wasn't too drunk to open it for business. I could mend boots with my eyes closed. I could put on heels and soles, then spray the inside with an aftershave lotion that made them smell brand-new. To this day I can put my fingers on a boot and tell if it's handmade or machine-made in one of those sweatshops where they turn out a thousand boots a day."

The old man was lying, stomach down, on a couch in his living room when we had this particular confabulation. His tunic was thrown over the back of a chair, the soft folds of bare skin on his bare back were covered with disgustingly bloated leeches sucking at his blood. "In your opinion, kid, what invention changed the world the most?" I remember him asking.

"That's easy," I said. "It has got to be the wheel. Or maybe Gutenberg's movable-type printing machine. Or the heavier-than-air flying machine."

"Wrong, wrong, and wrong again," he cried out like a schoolboy who had come up with the right answer. "The invention that changed the world, according to my sainted mother, was the button on your shirt. Imagine the first man—or given the fact it had to do with clothing, maybe it was the first woman—who had the ingenious idea of slipping a round object, the button in question, through a straight slit in the cloth, at which point the roundness of the button would assert itself and fasten the garment closed. What my mother was getting at was the genius of the human race that this demonstrated. Someone had to imagine it in their mind's eye before crafting it. A small round object. A straight slit. Once they invented the button, the rest was child's play: the wheel, Comrade Gutenberg's movable type, the heavier-than-air flying machine, which, by the way, was invented by a Russian—our very own Admiral Mozhaysky made the first steam-powered flight in 1884, which was nineteen years before the American Wright brothers managed to get their clumsy contraption off the ground."

"COLLECTIVIZATION RUINED STALIN'S REPUTA-tion," the old man, trembling in agitation, told me during another of my visits. I can still smell his breath drifting across the desk—it was especially sour that night. "To his everlasting credit," I remember him saying, "he swallowed the poison pill. Hang on my every word, kid, I'm going to give you the short course on the Bolshevik Revolution. So: There were actually two Revolutions in October of 1917, the one in the cities when the proletariat, along with soldiers exhausted by the war with Germany, rose up against the Provisional Government, the second in the countryside when the peasants chased off—and now and then murdered—their landlords. They divided up the great estates and began to farm them. Ten years after our Bolshevik Revolution, I'm not exaggerating, most of the tillable land in the Soviet Union was in private hands. Nobody—not Marx (who in a moment of candor once admitted he wasn't Marxist), not Lenin (who, with his notorious *one step back*, was not seriously Leninist), not Trotsky (who was a Menshevik before he saw which way the wind was blowing and joined the Bolsheviks), not Kamenev and Zinoviev (who were dead-set against launching our Bolshevik Revolution), certainly not the great coffeehouse intellectual Bukharin (who spent his waking hours trying to figure out how many Socialist angels could dance on the point of Hitler's dick)—none of them, not one, knew what to do about the hordes of unrepentant capitalists we called peasants. They weren't about to willingly give up their potsherd of land and two cows. Stalin—he is, let's face it, something of a genius, though as he is excruciatingly modest, he would be the first to deny it—grasped that Hitler would require *elbow room,* which made another European war inevitable. The existence in the West of the impenetrable Maginot Line, or if by some military miracle it was penetrated, the uncrossable English Channel, would oblige Hitler—cheered on by the sisters death and night, Roosevelt and Churchill—to turn east for what the Americans, with their Puritanical gift for muddying the water, justified as Manifest Destiny and the more straightforward Germans, calling a spade a spade, described as *elbow room.* Which would put the Red Army squarely in the Wehrmacht's path. Stalin took the view that we had ten years to catch up with the advanced industrial countries of Europe or perish. To industrialize, to create a steel industry from scratch, to build giant dams that provide electricity to our factories, to supply workers for these factories, we needed to transplant masses of peasants into the cities, and feed them. Which is why—the year, if memory isn't playing another of her tricks on me, was 1929—Stalin ordered the Bolshevik cadres into the countryside to organize the collectivization of agriculture. Do you understand the word *collectivization*, kid?"

"That they do teach at school," I said. "It's when a group of people pool their energies and their equipment for a common cause."

"The fucking peasants weren't about to pool the snot in their noses for a common cause," the old man said, making no effort to camouflage his bitterness. "They resisted viciously, slaughtering their livestock, burning their grain, letting their seeds rot. In 1930 alone they murdered a thousand Bolsheviks Stalin sent into the countryside to organize the collectives. In many ways the situation was more dangerous than the treacherous civil war that followed our Revolution. Back then we knew *who* our enemies were, we knew *where* our enemies were. We had the White armies attacking us, we had to deal with British troops in the north, French troops in the south and the Czech battalion that had occupied a big chunk of Siberia. For a while there, it was touch and go. If the Whites had triumphed, you can bet your sweet dipstick, all of us, starting with V. Lenin, would have been hanged by the neck until we croaked. Of course the Whites didn't triumph but collectivization was the civil war redux. You understand the word *redux*, kid? The weak-kneed pricks on the politburo thought Stalin would lose his nerve when famine spread to the Ukraine and the peasants were reduced to eating their children. I hope they cooked them first. Ha! Just joking. A few hundred thousand *kulaks* croaking, a few million Ukrainian peasants dying of famine wasn't pretty, I grant you, but it was the price we Bolsheviks had to pay for crash industrialization. The peasants, who know a thing or two about graveyards, say the death of one individual is a heartbreak, the death of one million is a statistic. Listen up, kid, hang on my words, the world, weaned on *realpolitik*, barely blinked when the British invented *concentration camps* and jam-packed them with Afrikaners after the Second Boer War. Where was the earsplitting outcry when the Turks exterminated a couple of million Armenians in 1915? Or when our very own Stalin rounded up and deported to the East a few hundred thousand Volga Germans at the start of the Great Patriotic War? When the kittens shed their crocodile tears over starving Ukrainians—it was enough to make a goddamn chicken laugh—Stalin instructed them that the Revolution was incapable of regretting. Stalin also instructed them that Red terror, to be effective, must be random. And under his inspired leadership, it was. The counter-revolutionists, the enemies of the people, the traitors, the conspirators went to sleep at night with a packed valise under their beds in case they woke up in a prison cell the next morning. It's no accident that Stalin's name means *steel*. Steel is what's in Stalin's spine. Collectivization was the solution to agricultural distribution, the solution to feeding the factory workers so Russia could mass-produce tanks and planes for the inevitable war against Nazi Germany. Stalin ordered ration cards in 1929, it helped but it didn't solve the shortages, so they were divided among the peasants."

"How can you divide shortages?"

It was dark out. The old man was standing in front of the only large window in his office, I couldn't tell if he was looking at his reflection in the glass or looking through it at the onion domes of a church. "Stalin swallowed the poison pill," he repeated.

"If the peasants were enemies of the people," I mumbled, "if they were criminals, if they were obstructing industrialization, I guess they needed to be arrested—"

The old man nodded so violently I thought he was going to throw his neck out. "Stalin could use someone like you on the politburo," he exclaimed, "a fresh face with a Communist's conscience to help defend the Revolution."

Think of it! Me, Leon Rozental, age ten and a half and a bit, the youngest member of Stalin's politburo! I'd need to have several copies of the glorious Soviet Constitution to sit on to reach the table. But, hey, why not?

I thought I heard a tinny gramophone playing the Communist *Internationale* in the giant ballroom below the old man's flat. Like every schoolboy in Russia, I knew the words by heart and sang out the first stanza along with the music: *Enslaved masses, stand up, stand up, the world is about to change.* When the old man angled his head to better hear me, I spotted an honest-to-goodness smile on his pasty face and a tear trickling from one of his squinty eyes. "You are the future, kid," he burst out. "We're infiltrated by counter-revolutionists, we're surrounded by enemies of the people, armies of them are trying to sabotage the Communist experiment before it can spread to the capitalist countries. Saboteurs are everywhere. Being late for work looks innocent enough, but being late for work three times constitutes sabotage and must be punished before it can infect the masses of workers. Did you know that counter-revolutionists have been caught throwing sand into fuel tanks, cut glass into bread dough? Which is why our CheKists are obliged to remain vigilant twenty-four hours a day, seven days a week. Only yesterday one of our CheKists, an honest policeman, a husband, a father, was found murdered in the House on the Embankment. His body was found floating in the swimming pool. Since you live in the Kremlin compound, I don't suppose you're familiar with the House on the Embankment. It's a viper's nest of counter-revolutionists. Dozens, even hundreds who live there have been arrested by our security organs. Sing those words again for me, kid."

I had trouble finding my voice. When I shut my eyes all I could see was the tiny hole in the back of Raincoat's neck. *Stand up, stand up, the world is about to change,* I managed to rasp.

I could tell the old man was pleased with me. He pulled one of his Herzegovina Flors from the pack and, peeling it open with a fingernail, packed the cigarette tobacco into the bowl of the meerschaum I'd given him. Sucking on the pipe, he lit it with a gold cigarette lighter he said the American President Roosevelt gave to esteemed Comrade Stalin when they met at Yalta. I noticed the old man's hand trembled as he held the flame to the bowl and looked away so as not to discomfort him. "Stalin doesn't get the credit he deserves," he said, his smoke-husky voice reaching me through the swirl of smoke. "All the coffeehouse intellectuals, starting with V. Lenin, including N. Bukharin and L. Trotsky and G. Zinoviev and L. Kamenev, were too busy jerking each other off with interpretations of this or that obscure Marxist doctrine while General Secretary Stalin put in fifteen-hour days organizing the Party so the Party could organize the country. When Lenin was alive and kicking, Stalin reported to him. When Lenin couldn't speak after his third stroke, that was in March of 1923, Stalin reported to himself. Listen, in their heart of hearts Lenin and Trotsky were sure the Russian Revolution wouldn't survive without another revolution in Europe. If it had been left to them, Russia would have played second fiddle to their grandiose plans for world revolution. It was Stalin who invented the formula *Communism in one country*. That country was Soviet Russia. It was Stalin who saved the Revolution. He was a hands-on ruler. He edited scripts for new films, he adjusted grain quotas depending on the region and the weather, he supervised the design and production of a new tank and a new fighter plane, he vetted staff appointments to district Soviets, he even found time to write a critique of Shostakovich's disgusting opera *Lady Macbeth of the Mtsensk District* for *Pravda*, for Christ's sake, though out of modesty, of course he signed it with a *nom de plume*. Do you understand the expression *nom de plume*? Doesn't matter if you don't. Did you know Lenin created the post of secretary general especially for Stalin? That's another little detail they don't teach in the schools. And then Lenin, on his deathbed, mind you, turned against Stalin because of a little spat he had with his wife. Do you understand what a spat is?"

I did actually. I used to lock myself in the bathroom and leave the water running in the sink to drown out my parents' voices when they quarrelled. "My father and mother had spats," I told Koba. "Sometimes they were not so little."

"Stalin, it can be said, has a bit of temper," he rambled on. "At one point he got exasperated with Krupskaya—just because she shit in the same toilet as Lenin didn't give her the right to badmouth the general secretary. Stalin told her if she didn't shut her trap he'd appoint a new wife for Lenin. The shrew scurried off to tattletale to the dying Lenin, who could barely talk but he could still write. Krupskaya's bitching got his attention. He scribbled a postscript to his last will and testament pissing on Stalin, telling the comrades that he was too rude to run the country, that he should be replaced. Stalin, too rude! Imagine. And replaced by whom? Nobody else wanted the fucking job. Stalin had to live with Lenin's slanderous postscript hanging over his head for years. Fact of the matter is the Bolshevik's clown prince didn't know what to make of Stalin. He never really figured him out. The general secretary wasn't an intellectual, he never pretended to be, but he was blessed with infallible gut instincts. I personally saw the two of them together on many occasions. Lenin wasn't comfortable in Stalin's presence, he was forever watching him out of the corner of his eye to monitor his reaction. You can bet the illustrious Karl Heinrich Marx must be turning over in his London grave at the thought that the leader of the world Communist movement doesn't swallow all of his *Das Kapital* bullcrap. Religion may be, as Marx preached, the opiate of the masses, but in the first months of the Great Patriotic War, when it looked as if nothing could stop the German invaders, when the Wehrmacht came within shouting distance of Moscow before the Red Army and Father Winter were able to knock the socks off them, the opium poppy, not Marxism, was the opiate of choice of

Joseph Stalin. It's what kept him sane when the defeatists around him were asylum-bound. You didn't ask for it but I'll give you my opinion, kid. When the historians get around to writing about the Revolution and the Civil War and Lenin and Stalin, they will comprehend the inconvenient truth, which is that Lenin was jealous of Stalin. Maybe Lenin's Jew blood was at the root of this jealousy. You can bet our history books don't mention that Lenin had Jew blood. He himself never admitted it. It was a state secret, swept under the carpet. I have it on good authority his maternal grandfather was a Ukrainian Yid who converted in order to escape the Jewish Pale of Settlement and get into university. My god, if you think Stalin had a temper, you should have seen Lenin explode. He could fly into a tantrum over the most trivial things. I was in the room once when he lambasted a barber because he didn't like the way he cut his hair. Lenin had small ugly lily-soft hands, nobody remarked it but me, the kittens were hostage to his legend. You know what they say about small hands—"

"Small hands, small gloves," I said brightly.

"Whatever. Fact is, Lenin wasn't very courageous. When the rest of us were out in the Petrograd streets battling the Provisional Government, the great helmsman of the Revolution, as Lenin styled himself, hid out in Smolny, the swanky girl's school we requisitioned as an HQ. Ha! Lenin's problem, the problem of all those preening coffee-house brainboxes, was they were intoxicated by European culture. They loathed Stalin as an incarnation of ignorant Asiatic Russia. Listen, the coffeehouse clique may have helped stir up revolution but they never thought beyond the Revolution. That shit job they left to Stalin. He was the one who fit all those little screws onto the great locomotive so that the wheels turned when it dragged the state down the tracks."

The telephone on Koba's desk jingled. Observably annoyed at the interruption, he plucked the receiver off the hook and listened for a moment. I had spent enough time with him to tell he was vexed, so I wasn't flabbergasted when he snapped at the person who had the misfortune to be on the other end of the line. "On the matter of *Onegin*, which Stalin attended last night, he was overheard saying he found it outrageous that Tatiana appeared onstage in a sheer gown. Don't interrupt me, goddamn it. No, I am not giving instructions, I am merely passing on a casual comment of Stalin's. It's up to you to figure out what he meant. It is up to you to figure out what to do."

Leon speaking: I need to admit I didn't know who this Comrade *Onegin* was. I hope I spelled his name right.

Hanging down the receiver, the old man's attention turned to the sheaf of papers on his blotter. From my side of the desk I could only see the pages upside down, but they appeared to be filled with long lists of names—surname, given name, patronymic. Fitting on a pair of spectacles, snatching up a fountain pen, Koba bent over the sheaf and began to scribble *za* in red ink in the upper right-hand corner of each page. I supposed the list listed members of the Party who were eligible for promotions or pensions or military decorations or hard-to-get Moscow residence permits. Hey, maybe even passports so they could travel abroad. Why else would someone as important as Koba waste his precious time approving lists? Now and then a particular name seemed to catch his eye and he would scratch a line through it—no promotion, no passport for that person! Or did I get it backward? Was the list a list of enemies of the people to be punished for one thing or another, and the ones with lines through their names, because the old man knew them personally, were to be left unpunished? Either or, it proved that my newfound friend Koba was someone to reckon with.

When the old man finished initialling the pages he suddenly remembered I was in the room. "You still here? Where was I?"

"You were giving me a short course on the Bolshevik Revolution."

"So: There were actually two Revolutions in October of 1917, the one in the cities when the proletariat, along with soldiers exhausted by the war—"

I held up a hand the way we were taught to in school when we wanted to get a word in edgewise. "What?" he asked.

"You told me that already," I said.

The old man appeared confused. "When?"

"A few minutes ago."

"Did I? Oh." And, funnily, he began to sing in the deep-throated voice of a priest. *Gospodi pomilui, gospodi pomilui, gospodi pomilui.*

"On who should the Lord have mercy?" I asked.

"On me."

"But I thought you didn't believe in god."

The old man swallowed a laugh. "Asking the Lord who may or may not exist to have mercy on you should be seen as a life insurance policy."

"THEY FOUND THE BODY," PAVEL WHISPERED TO me. "I saw them from my window loading it into an ambulance. Police cars blocked the street outside. There were raincoats as far as the eye could see. Are you sure they won't find the rug and the pistol?"

I'd loaded a fifth bullet into my mother's Chagan and stashed it back behind the books, we'd sponged the foam that had seeped from the dead man's lips off the Indian rug and hidden it under a bigger rug in Zinaida's parents' bathroom. Still, us kids were jumpy. I suppose you could say we were all seriously nervous about not living long enough to become adults.

IN MY DREAM, I'M SITTING ON TWO COPIES OF THE glorious Soviet Constitution and *The Twelve Sexual Commandments of the Proletariat* so I can reach the table. I'm wearing the knee-length white pants and the navy jumper my parents bought for me when we vacationed at the government guesthouse for physicists on the Black Sea the summer before my dad's death. The old man, sitting on my right, is wearing a military tunic crawling with the medals he keeps fetching from a shoebox and pinning on—before he can pin on a new one he has to take an old one off to make room for it. Esteemed Comrade Stalin, bending under the weight of the gold braid on his marshal's uniform, presides, not from the head of the table but from the seat just to the right.

The short man with the monocle who pinned that medal on my mother's breast sits at the head of the table puffing away on an American Lucky Strike cigarette (which, as I speak American, I recognize to be an expression from their decadent national sport, base ball). "The first order of business," esteemed Comrade Stalin announces in my dream, "is to welcome the newest politburo member to our ranks. His name"—he sneaks a quick look at an index card on the table in front of him—"is Leon Rozental, age ten and a half—"

"And two days," I correct him from my place at the table.

Esteemed Comrade Stalin chuckles amiably. "Ten and a half and two days," he says. He aims a grandfatherly grin in my direction. "Leon here is the son of the late Hero of the Soviet Union, the physicist Rozental, who saved the uranium rods when counter-revolutionists attempted to sabotage the first Soviet chain reaction."

The men around the table applaud. It takes me a lifetime to realize they are applauding me. The old man nudges my rib cage. "Stand up and take a bow," he hisses.

And I do. I stand up and I bow from the waist.

In my dream, esteemed Comrade Stalin notices the label of my jumper is on the outside, which means I'm wearing it inside out.

"Your sweater is inside out," he remarks.

"His sweater is inside out," Lucky Strike agrees.

"I know," I say.

Esteemed Comrade Stalin is intrigued. "You know and you still wear it that way?"

"My dad had this fetish—he always wore his sweaters inside out. He said it was because the world was inside out. I'm too young to know what he meant by that, though you, being the heritor apparent of esteemed Comrade Lenin, can probably figure it out."

"Your father undoubtedly meant the capitalist world was inside out," I hear esteemed Comrade Stalin say. "Our Communist world is obviously the opposite—outside in." Around the table heads nod in eager agreement.

"But . . . but outside in is the same as—" I start to say when Lucky Strike interrupts me from the head of the table. "Precisely what is your area of expertise?" he demands, the soggy American cigarette glued to his lower lip.

"I'm an expert on kid-hood," I tell him. "As the only genuine kid on the politburo, I will make it my job to represent the interests of children."

"And what," esteemed Comrade Stalin asks, "is the main problem confronting children in our workers' paradise?"

I turn to speak to esteemed Comrade Stalin directly. "The main problem for children today is the arrest of parents."

There is an angry murmur from the men around the table. One of the kittens—to my amazement it's none other than the doorman from the House on the Embankment, in full admiral's regalia, gold epaulets and all—furiously scrapes back his chair and stalks from the room. Esteemed Comrade Stalin frowns at me in annoyance. "The security organs have their area of expertise," he says, "and we in the politburo have ours. The two do not overlap. We run the country, the security organs protect it from traitors and counter-revolutionists. The arrest of parents, assuming such arrests really take place, have absolutely nothing to do with the comrades in this room."

The old man sitting next to me stands up to address esteemed Comrade Stalin. "I ask the general secretary to excuse my young friend," he says. "Leon here has no experience in politburo protocol—" The old man nudges my ribs again and stage-whispers to me, "Do you understand the word *protocol*?"

I didn't but I was not about to admit my ignorance in the presence of esteemed Comrade Stalin.

I suddenly realize that the Uzbek cook with the ski-slope nose and slanty eyes is also a member of the politburo. He climbs to his feet and stabs a finger at me across the table. "He does not eat his vegetables," he says accusingly. "Whether or not he asks for vegetables, I always make it a point to put a portion on his tray, but he pushes them to one side and leaves them over. Starving peasants in the Ukraine are eating their children but this kid who lives in the lap of luxury in the House on the Embankment does not eat his vegetables. It is not Soviet."

"That was the first thing I asked him when he turned up in the compound," the old man tells esteemed Comrade Stalin. "Did he eat his vegetables? In his defense, he answered honestly. He said not when he can not."

The general secretary is not happy with the newest member of the politburo. "Honesty cannot save him if he doesn't eat his vegetables," esteemed Comrade Stalin announces. "If found guilty, the penalty will be weeks, even months on his way to Siberia in a cattle car without a flush toilet, not to mention a canteen. He will be deported wearing the clothes he is dressed in now."

The thought of winding up on the icicle-crusted steppes of Siberia shivering in short pants and an inside-out jumper, with my pee-pee freezing before it hits the ground, is enough to scare me awake. It takes me a moment to remember who I am and where I am not. Where I am not is Siberia. Lying on the cot in my secret room, I gulp air into my lungs, relieved to discover it has all been a bad dream.

Usually I counted my blessings on the fingers of my left hand. After the dream I added one finger from my right hand—thank goodness I'm not a member of the politburo.

ISABEAU WAS FURIOUS WITH ME WHEN I TOLD HER about the politburo meeting. "In my opinion, which I more or less agree with, it was pretty dumb, even for you," she said. "Even in a dream you got to be careful what you say and who you say it to."

"In my defense, when I said it, I didn't know I was inside a dream. I thought I was a member of the politburo."

"In your defense, considering you couldn't know you were inside a dream while you were actually inside the dream in question, you were pretty gosh-awful brave to raise the arrest of parents." Isabeau started to giggle. "The Uzbek cook from the canteen being a member of the politburo—that's rich. And accusing you of not eating your vegetables in front of Comrade Stalin!" Suddenly she looked at me funnily. "How come the Uzbek was in your dream and I wasn't?"

I had to think fast. "Consider the probability I was protecting you by keeping you out of my dream."

Isabeau thought about that for a moment. She nodded to indicate she had processed this information. Then, smiling a scrumptiously naughty smile, she leaned over and kissed me. On the lips.

It was the first time a live human girl had kissed me on the lips. That and my dad's death and my mom's arrest were so far the major events in my life.

I REMEMBER ASKING THE OLD MAN, SOON AFTER I had this dream of being in Stalin's politburo, if he remembered his dreams.

Believe it or not, "I don't sleep long enough to dream" was his answer. "The few nights I do, I probably dream dreams but I try not to remember them."

"Why? What are you afraid of?"

"Listen carefully, kid, copy what I say into that notebook of yours when you get home, it may come in handy when you write my authorized biography. When I was younger I would wake up in the morning in a cold sweat, scrambling to get myself back into a dream I could only half remember. But as I got older—as I got *old*—I saw the advantage of letting it slip through my fingers. You aren't obliged to decipher dreams you can't get back into. In this, as in most things, Stalin is my role model. When he was the commissar in charge of Volgograd during our civil war, he decided to make an example of a few dozen White Russian officers—he ordered our soldiers to bind the prisoners' ankles and wrists and push them off barges into the Volga. I have heard Stalin ruminate about this episode. I heard him say he needed to purge it from his dream bank to have a hope in hell of getting on with his life."

The old man ignited a new Herzegovina Flor on the embers of the one that had burned down dangerously close to his lips. "In our brain," I heard him murmur, "we are all serving life sentences for crimes we don't remember committing."

I copied the sentence into my notebook as soon as I got home and read it from time to time without really understanding what he meant. Maybe I will one day. Maybe I won't.

ONE EVENING THE GUARDS STANDING AROUND the chessboard spotted me coming across the ballroom. The Chief in a civilian suit glared at me as if I might be a burglar and muttered something about me needing to wait downstairs because the *Vozhd* was holding a meeting of the politburo in his apartment. *The politburo*, no less! This proved, if I'd had any doubts, which I didn't, that he really did help esteemed Comrade Stalin run the country. I ended up playing black while I waited but my mind wasn't on the game and I missed a fatal attack by white's king's bishop that left my opponent, the Chief himself, smirking with pleasure as he wiped me off the board. I was going to concede when the door at the top of the winding metal staircase opened and a dozen or so men trooped out. The guards, including my opponent, stood to attention as they passed so I knew these guys must have been important. I recognized one from a poster I'd seen in the subway—his name was Nikita something or other, he was a Hero of the Soviet Union for organizing the construction of our amazing Moscow metro system. Another guy actually nodded at me as he passed. I recognized him too, he was the short man with a monocle glued to one eye who had pinned the medal on my mom's dress after my dad's death. When I finally made it upstairs, I found the old man hunched over his desk, carefully counting out drops into a glass of water from an eyedropper.

"Eight, nine, ten," he murmured.

"You got ulcers or something?" I asked. I knew about ulcers because my dad complained of ulcers before radiation poisoning murdered him.

My innocent question seemed to annoy Koba. "I don't *get* ulcers," he snapped. "I *give* ulcers." He threw his head back and drank off the concoction in several long gulps. "Ughhh," he said, grimacing. "I hate the taste. It's not medicine, it's a cure. The peasants in the mountains of Abkhazia, which is a part of my native Georgia, live long lives thanks to two daily doses of tincture of iodine in a glass filled with pure mountain water. So we ship bottles of this water, which comes from melting glaciers high up in the Caucasus, to the Kremlin every day. There's a woman in Abkhazia who is said to be one hundred and twenty-nine years old, there's a man who claims to be even older and has proposed marriage to her. Stalin just signed a letter congratulating him on his hundred and thirtieth birthday. I envy him his erections, assuming he still has them."

"If your doctors think this iodine treatment works, maybe I should try it."

"I don't trust the fucking doctors," the old man said. "I don't trust their fucking hospitals either." He stuck a fingernail into an ear and scratched at it, mining wax. "What do they know about bloody flux or Saint Anthony's fire?" he demanded. "The way I see it, the dumbest peasant knows ten times more than the smartest doctor. My sainted mother, Keke, thought garlic could cure seven diseases, which is why to this day I wear a necklace of cloves around my neck. Keke taught me the body has four humors. It's when they became unbalanced that you get sick."

I was thinking what my mother would say if I told her garlic cures seven diseases or the body has four humors, whatever those were. "So how can you tell when the body is unbalanced?" I asked.

"You look at the piss," Koba explained. "I myself always piss into a milk bottle so I can check the color and consistency."

"And if there is an unbalance?"

"Small doses of camphor usually set things right. A boar's bile enema is excellent for chronic constipation. Hedgehog grease cures lumbago. It's well known that leeching can relieve the ache of rheumatism in your joints."

"Where do you find leeches in Moscow?"

"I have them flown in from the Vasyugan Swamp near Omsk in Siberia," he explained. "The leeches from there are thirsty little fuckers," he added with a laugh. "You ask a lot of questions for a kid. You planning to be a doctor when you grow up?"

"I'm not positive I'll get to grow up," I heard myself say, and I knew instantly this is what I believed. "If by some freak twist of fate I manage to survive kid-hood, I plan to work on the thing that stumped Einstein, which is finding a unified field theory that explains relativity, electromagnetism, gravitation, and quantum mechanics. I plan to figure out how this strange universe we find ourselves in evolved, after the big bang, from an ultra-high compression where all the galaxies were crushed into a space smaller than a camphor ball."

"You really are a smart-ass, kid, aren't you? Where did you pick up all that stuff? At school?"

"They don't teach these things at school, Koba—not to kids, at least. I learned about relativity, electromagnetism, gravitation, quantum mechanics, particle physics, non-Euclidean geometry, the way babies learn Russian. It was in the air I breathed at home. It was in the books my dad brought home for me to read, starting, when I was eight and a quarter, with Aristotle's *Physica*. I also taught myself to speak American and I'm working on Arabic. Once I read something I don't forget it. Ever. I can name all the bones in the human body. I read a book about ants. It said an ant had a single fiber for a brain, but that two ants circling a dead butterfly looked an awful lot like an idea. My dad said two bombers circling a city looked like an idea gone wrong, but that's a whole other story. My dad once told me, at the rate I was going, I could apply to Moscow State University when I reached thirteen. Hey, if I somehow reach thirteen I'd love to go to university. Most of the girls there probably have breasts."

"When I was your age the only thing in the air was the smell of vodka on my father's breath at home and the smell of leather in his shoe shop." He shut one eye and looked at me with the other. I had the creepy feeling he was taking aim. "What makes you think you won't get to grow up?"

"My mom's been arrested. There are rumors that the kids of arrested people are also arrestable."

The old man was suddenly all ears. "Why was your mother arrested?"

"I don't know. When they arrested her they never said."

"You were there when she was arrested!"

"Sort of. Yes. I saw them search our apartment. I saw them take her away."

The old man switched on a headlight in his open eye. His nostrils twitched as if he smelled trouble. "What's your mother's name, kid?"

"Rozental, Anastasia Andreevna."

"OKAY, CALM DOWN AND TELL ME EXACTLY WHAT you told this old man of yours," Isabeau ordered.

"So you believe me, you believe I talk to this old man who helps esteemed Comrade Stalin run the country?"

"You're not answering my question."

"You're not answering mine."

"Let's say, for argument's sake, your old man is not a figment of your imagination."

"Let's," I agreed. I had the awful feeling in my stomach that Isabeau would think I had betrayed my mom. "He wanted to know my mother's name."

"And you told him?"

"I thought maybe he could help somehow—"

"And could he? Can he? Did he?"

I need to admit here that I was walking the fine line between bursting into tears and passing out completely. "The next time I saw him—"

"Which was when?"

"Two nights ago. He was sitting on the bottom rung of the winding staircase, both his hands wrapped around his glass of warm milk, waiting for me. There were crumbs on his tunic from the *churek* he'd been nibbling. The four policemen were standing with their backs to the wall next to where they leaned their rifles."

"And?"

"And he said to me—"

"Spit it out, Leon."

"He told me he, like esteemed Comrade Stalin, normally had no contact with the security organs but that he had made an exception for me. He told me he had phoned up someone who knew someone who worked in the NKVD archive department. And that someone had looked up my mother's name and . . ."

"And?"

"And that she has confessed."

"Oh dear god, Leon! Confessed to what?"

"Confessed to conspiring with other doctors in the Kremlin hospital to hurt esteemed Comrade Stalin, him and other members of the politburo."

"Hurt how? How hurt?"

"The old man didn't say hurt. He said . . . kill. Or maybe he said murder. Or poison."

"What did you say when he said that?"

"I . . . I laughed."

"You what!"

"I didn't know what to say. So I laughed. And when the four guys leaning against the wall heard me laughing, they laughed. And when the old man heard them laughing, he laughed too. And we were all laughing because . . . because my mother had confessed to wanting to poison esteemed Comrade Stalin."

"How could you laugh at that?"

Knowing me, I'm pretty sure I must have shrugged. "It was either laugh or cry. And I didn't want all those grown-ups to see me cry and think, hey, he's just a kid after all."

SIX

WHERE ISABEAU ENTERTAINS THE POSSIBILITY THE KID MAY BE TELLING THE TRUTH

FROM LEON'S NOTEBOOK:

ME: My father, my mother brought me up to love Soviet power.

THE OLD MAN: It is not enough to love Soviet power. Soviet power has to love you. (He lifts his nightshirt and begins harvesting lint from his belly button as he crafts one of his befuddling afterthoughts.) Listen carefully, kid, memorize what I'm about to tell you, write it down when you get home. *No chain is stronger than its weakest link* (is what he finally comes up with when he runs out of lint).

ME: Can you repeat that?

THE OLD MAN: No.

I sense that his *Soviet power has to love you* and his *No chain is stronger than its weakest link* are related, but I'm not sure how. Yet.

S O I NEED TO GO THERE, HOWEVER UNCOM-fortable it makes me feel. Here's the thing: I'm starting to think Leon's story about talking to an old man who lives above an airplane hangar could be, might be, well—how can I say this?—factual as opposed to fictional. I mean, there are so many details even Leon, who is famous in kid circles at the House on the Embankment for his wild imagination—he thinks the doorman downstairs is really an admiral in the Soviet navy—couldn't invent them. How could he possibly know the name of esteemed Vladimir Lenin's lady friend? How could Leon know he even had a lady friend or that she was French? There's no way he would have made up the story about his mother confessing to trying to poison General Secretary Stalin. And what about those packets of rubles bound in rubber bands? Where the heck did they come from if it wasn't an old man living above the airplane hangar who gave them to him? Answer me that. And then there are all those details about Comrade Stalin and the Great Patriotic War. How could Leon know all that stuff if he didn't get it from this old man who helps Comrade Stalin run the country?

As far back as I can remember, the Great Patriotic War was table talk in my house, which is understandable considering my father was a historian specializing in the subject. His doctoral thesis at Moscow State University, where he held a full professorship when he was only thirty-six—"Premature Anti-Fascism: Capitalist Hypocrisy in Trying to Push Joseph Stalin into War against Adolf Hitler at the time of the 1939 Soviet-German Non-Aggression Pact"—was published as a book a year before my dad's arrest and, eh, execution as a British spy. (Peculiarly, copies are still on sale in the two Moscow book stores I visited with my mother before *her* arrest. My mom bought one of them to give to a friend but the raincoats arrested the book, along with my mother, before she got the chance.) All of which is to say that, though I'm only 4,046 days old, which is eleven years one month and four days in adult-speak, stories about the Great Patriotic War have always fascinated me. I could describe the entire battle of Stalingrad by the time I was seven. When I was nine I wrote an essay about Soviet tactics in the great tank battles on the Kursk steppe. One of my earliest memories—it was 1945, I was only three at the time—was when my father took me to see our glorious Red Army soldiers parading through Red Square to celebrate the German surrender. I have this picture in my brain of them flinging dozens upon dozens of captured Nazi battle banners at the foot of Lenin's tomb while Comrade Stalin—my father pointed him out, he was the small figure in an Army greatcoat on the reviewing stand—waved his approval.

Here are some of the things the old man told Leon about Comrade Stalin and the Great Patriotic War:

1. Hitler planned to invade the Soviet Union in the middle of May 1941—he picked this date because the Russian peasants would have sowed their grain but the crops would have been too small to burn and the Germans could have confiscated the eventual harvest. But Hitler made the dumb mistake of trying to conquer Greece and Yugoslavia first, which set back his attack on the Soviet Union for five precious weeks, allowing winter to set in before his divisions could reach Moscow. Luckily for us, Russian winter was ready for the Wehrmacht but the Wehrmacht wasn't ready for Russian winter. They didn't have winter lubricants for their rifles or their tanks. Soviet soldiers had been issued American-made felt boots two sizes too big so they could stuff them with newspaper. German soldiers had been issued boots to fit their Teutonic feet, which is how come tens of thousands of them suffered frostbite and had to have tens of thousands of toes amputated.

2. Hitler massed 153 divisions for his attack on the Soviet Union. According to Leon's old man, Comrade Stalin's generals begged him to defend the frontiers, which would have meant committing Russian reserves in the opening days of the war. But Comrade Stalin, who claimed to understand military strategy better than his generals, decided to take a page from the plan used by the one-eyed Marshal Kutuzov to defeat Napoleon when *he* made the fatal mistake of invading Russia. Kutuzov ordered his armies to retreat before Napoleon, luring him deeper and deeper into Russia, which meant his supply lines got longer and longer. Comrade Stalin made the Germans pay dearly for every village and town they captured as they drove deep into the Soviet Union, but he stubbornly kept his reserves in reserve—and it was these reserve divisions that turned the tide when Russian winter set in. Unlike Napoleon, Hitler never did capture Moscow.

3. The old man even defended Comrade Stalin's decision to sign the non-aggression pact with Hitler's foreign minister Ribbentrop in 1939 on the grounds that it bought time to start production of the new tank that was better than the German Panzers, time to perfect a new fighter plane that could outmaneuver anything the Luftwaffe could put into the air. (The old man dropped an intimate detail into the story—that Stalin always referred to Ribbentrop using Hitler's pet name for his foreign minister, which was *the little champagne salesman*.) The non-aggression pact gave the Soviet Union breathing space—it moved the Soviet frontier hundreds of kilometers into Europe, which put Leningrad way back inside Soviet territory.

Speaking as my father's daughter, I can say all of these details ring true, but it's not something my bosom buddy Leon—who is, I am the first to admit, pretty neat when it comes to explaining Einstein's relativity and quantum mechanics—would be capable of inventing.

Which makes the old man living above a hangar-sized ballroom flesh-and-blood real, right?

Maybe.

SEVEN

WHERE THE KID TRIES TO TEACH THE OLD MAN TO PLAY CHESS

FROM LEON'S NOTEBOOK:

THE OLD MAN: I'll let you in on a state secret, kid. Too much peace and quiet gives Stalin a migraine, it reminds him of when his father was too drunk to talk to his mother and his mother was too angry to answer him if he did. Which is why he personally feels obliged to fill any lull in the conversation. Very occasionally he has been known to do it with a joke. (Coughing up a laugh.) He told a beauty the other night—I have to admit it had his kittens in stitches. The hilarious part is that Stalin told a joke about Stalin.

ME: I thought it was against the law to tell jokes about esteemed Comrade Stalin.

THE OLD MAN: It is. But there's an exemption if the person telling the joke about Stalin is Stalin. You want to hear the joke or not, kid?

ME: If it's against the law to tell a joke about Stalin, it's probably against the law to listen to a joke about Stalin.

THE OLD MAN: Being that you're only a kid, you'll get an exemption too. Here's the joke. Stalin's old mother visits him in the Kremlin and he shows her around his apartment—there are eight rooms, every second room has a tiled stove, there are three bathrooms with running hot water and flush toilets, there are servants to make the beds and serve the meals, there's even a sauna. His old mother isn't impressed. So Stalin takes her to his house on the Lenin Hills—there are fourteen rooms, each room is equipped with a tiled stove, there are so many servants they have their own kitchen, there's central heating, there's an American Jacuzzi in the bathroom and a twenty-seat movie theatre in the basement. His mother isn't impressed. So he flies her by helicopter to his dacha in the woods at Kuntsevo, which he calls the Near Dacha because he has other dachas further from Moscow, and he gives her a tour of the estate in his American Cadillac car. There are two-hundred acres of fields and woods next to a winding river, there are twenty rooms in the main house including a sixty-seat movie theatre, there are heated indoor and outdoor swimming pools and a solarium, there's central heating in the winter and air-conditioning in the summer, the kitchen is equipped with an American Formica counter and a walk-in refrigerator. His mother, still not impressed, warns, Son, what if the Reds should come? So how is it you're not laughing, kid? Are you too thick to get it? What if the Reds should come? We're the Reds, god damn it! We already came.

ME: I'm not sure esteemed Comrade Stalin's joke is a laughing matter.

"NO, NO, NOT LIKE THAT, HOW MANY TIMES do I have to tell you the bishop can't jump over the pawn like a horse. You need to first move the pawn out of his way to bring the bishop into play."

"The bishop moves diagonally one square at a time?"

"Diagonally as many squares as you want."

"I thought the queen moves diagonally as many squares as you want."

"She does. She moves like a bishop if she wants to. She also moves like a rook, sideways or up and back. And as many squares as she wants."

"So I ought to think of the queen as a rook and a bishop combined. Can she move like the horse too?"

"How about we take a break," I suggested.

The old man, his lips pursed, his eyes squinting, sat staring irritably at the board. If looks could kill, the Chinese chessmen would be dead. "Fuck this," I remember him muttering under his breath. "I get how capitalist kings and queens and bishops move around Europe better than how these slant-eyed chessmen move around this chessboard."

I'd hijacked the ivory Chinese chessmen from the bodyguards in the hangar downstairs and was trying to teach the old man the fundamentals of the game—how the different pieces moved, how you took advantage of their peculiar quirks to concentrate your forces and mount an attack, how you sacrificed a pawn or a knight to bait a trap, how you retreated behind a phalanx of pawns to mount a defense. Maybe it was because chess reminded him of Siberia, maybe he was prejudiced against Chinese, maybe it was just plain thick-headedness, maybe it was all of the above. Obviously chess was not the old man's glass of tea.

Valechka turned up with a bowl of ice cream for me and a glass of warm milk for the old man. I have to report his hand trembled as he drank it, causing some of the milk to spill onto his tunic. I pretended not to notice. I was digging into my ice cream and, to make confabulation, asked him if he ever did sports.

"Didn't your parents teach you not to talk with your mouth full?" he growled.

"If you keep picking on the young man, Joseph, he's not going to want to come back," Valechka said. (She sounded exactly like my mom telling my dad not to be too hard on the kid.) On her way out, Valechka called over her shoulder to me, "Don't mind him—he's a crotchety old man living in a bubble."

He waved to her and tapped his wristwatch with a fingernail. Smiling, she nodded in agreement. He turned back to me. "To answer your question," he said. "If you consider robbing banks a sport, sure, I did sports. In my day Georgia was like the Wild West of America—I'd hitch a horse to the fence behind the bank, then stand on the saddle and cut the telephone wire before bursting through the back door with one of my beautiful pearl-handled revolvers in each fist. Oh, you should have seen the look on the face of the terrified tellers! They'd throw the cash from the safe into mail sacks and I'd gallop out of town before the tsar's fat constables discovered the money in the bank had been liberated."

"Hey, like, I meant real sports like soccer or wrestling or one-two-three ring relievo."

I remember the old man sucking thoughtfully on his cigarette before coming up with an answer. "Once, when I was five or six, there was this pyramid contest between Gori, where I lived, and Baku. The men dressed in different-color clothing: Gori was red, Baku was green. And the idea was to build a human pyramid with the strongest men on the bottom, then the next strongest climbed onto their shoulders, and so on until the pyramid was five levels high. And then I, being the lightest and the most agile kid in town, scrambled up the pyramid, my foot in the belts and on the shoulders of the men, until I was on top of everyone. I was level six. And I'd stand up and raise my arms over my head and the whole town cheered me. I can say I loved being on top of the pyramid." At which point Koba, talking more to himself than to me, said something that didn't make much sense but I repeat it anyhow. "I still love being on top of the pyramid."

I HAVE THIS REMEMBRANCE OF THE OLD MAN COM-plaining one night about not being able to fall asleep. He told me he slept on the heart side, which was one of his mother's bromides that was said to tire out the heart and help you drift off into sleep, though his sleep, when it finally came, only brought with it a tangle of interlocking nightmares. The old man said something about preferring nightmares to day-mares. I asked him to explain the difference. I got the feeling he was swallowing my question as if it was something that needed to be digested before he could come back at me with an answer. "Nightmares you wake up from and, *pfffft*, they're behind you even if your pyjamas are still damp from sweat," is what I remember him finally saying. "There's no *pfffft* with day-mares—you have to live with them every hour of every day."

As the old man was one of esteemed Comrade Stalin's close comrades, I asked if the esteemed general secretary had trouble falling asleep, what with the weight of the world being on his shoulders and all. I wrote down what I could remember of his answer in my notebook: "Stalin's nightmares and day-mares are pretty much the same. At night he dreams he's surrounded by Jews—you have to remember the Russian Socialist movement was crawling with Jew intellectuals. When he wakes up, which is invariably before dawn, he *is* surrounded by Jews. In the early days after the Revolution there was Trotsky, whose Jew name was Bronshtein, there was Zinoviev, whose Jew name was Apfelbaum, there was Kamenev, whose Jew name was Rozenfeld, there was Lazar Kaganovich, who we called to his face *Kosherovich*. They were the advance guard of the international Jew conspiracy. The guy who wrote the Communist Manifesto, for Christ's sake, the illustrious Karl Marx, was the grandson of a goddamn rabbi. Stalin's daughter, Svetlana, lost her virginity to a Jew actor when she was sixteen and he was almost forty. When Stalin pinned a Siberian tenner on him she found herself another Jew lover, only this one she married. Fortunately the marriage didn't last long. Stalin's son Yakov married a Jewess named Yulia, he tried to talk him out of it but Yakov was like his father when he sets his mind on something, and in the end a man loves the woman he loves. I have to admit the Jewess was a hot number; she had this way of dancing with her head thrown back and her large breasts bouncing under her peasant blouse. Eventually Stalin realized there was nothing to be done about Jews plaguing his nightmares except sleep less, but he decided to purge the Jews from his day-mares. The peasants have a saying: *Little strokes fell great oaks!* Trotsky, with his devil's pointed beard, was the first great oak to fall. He was not invited to attend Lenin's funeral, his minions in the Party were quietly sidelined, then he himself was expelled from the Party. Eventually he was expelled from the country, he took refuge in Mexico thinking he'd be safe there from Stalin's long arm—until an agent from the NKVD's Special Tasks planted an ice axe in his skull. Ha! Trotsky had the gall to slander Stalin, calling him the gravedigger of the revolution. Stalin was a gravedigger, alright, but the grave he dug was Trotsky's! Trotsky had company in the Bolshevik graveyard. When Zinoviev and Kamenev were arrested, that was in the 1930s, Stalin personally met with them and promised their lives would be spared if they confessed their treason at a public trial. The bastards wanted him to put the promise in writing. *Are you saying you don't trust me?* Stalin demanded. If the judge decided to have them shot despite their confessions and Stalin's promise, it clearly wasn't Stalin's fault—he was a simple comrade in the service of the Party, one of many—he had nothing to do with how the wheels of justice turned. Stalin's day-mares became known to the security organs. Thinking to suck up to him they even arrested the Jew wives of two politburo kittens, Molotov and Voroshilov. To paraphrase the peasants, the ladies in question were guilty until proven innocent. The hard truth is that Stalin always considered Soviet Jews to be a fifth column. You comprehend the expression *fifth column*, kid? It comes from the Spanish civil war, and refers to traitors living on your side of the battle line who will rise up and stab you in the back. I'll let you in on a little state secret—don't repeat it to a soul, living or dead. The secretary general thinks Hitler was on to something with his *Juden*-free model. So it's not surprising Stalin is working on a plan along those lines. He's going to deport the Jews, all two million of the paragraph-five motherfuckers, to Birobidzhan, deep in Siberia near the Chinese border. He has decided it will be easier to keep track of these ideological saboteurs if they're all in the same basket. The goddamn Zionists have wet dreams of a new Galilee. Stalin will give them a new Galilee *eight thousand kilometers due east of Moscow.* Jewish nationalism, which is another name for Zionism, is the root problem— scratch a Jew, you uncover a Zionist, scratch a Zionist, you uncover a British spy. Listen, kid, Russian Jews don't pledge allegiance to Stalin and the Soviet Union, they pledge allegiance to some godforsaken holy wasteland in the middle of a sea of Arabs. It's not a coincidence that these same Zionists want to rewrite the history of the Great Patriotic War. They claim the Germans murdered Jews when anyone who takes the trouble to understand the so-called Holocaust *dialectically* knows the Germans murdered *Russians*, some of whom happened to be Jews. The organs recently arrested Jew doctors working in the Kremlin hospital. They were part of a Zionist conspiracy to murder Soviet leaders, starting with Stalin himself. Ha! Speaking of day-mares, Stalin once saw the Jew actor Shloyme Mikhoels play King Lear. One reviewer wrote Mikhoels didn't *act* Lear, he *became* Lear. I happened to be at the theatre with Stalin that evening. I saw Mikhoels become Lear, more to the point I saw *Lear* become *Stalin*. Stalin's not blind. He saw Lear become Stalin too, and he wasn't happy about it because Stalin doesn't see himself as Lear, the manic despot who made the stupid blunder of giving up power too soon. He sees himself as Peter the Great. He sees himself as Ivan Grozny, Russia's first tsar known to the world as Ivan the Dread. He sees himself as Genghis Khan leading his Mongol hordes out of Asia across the Kara-Kum desert to conquer Urgench in Turkmenistan. Though you have to wonder why the hell Genghis Khan wanted Urgench. I spent seven months hiding from the tsar's police in that shithole of a town. I can tell you there were days when I would have preferred a prison in Siberia. Talk about coincidence, I heard our CheKists found Mikhoels's body in a snowdrift in Minsk not long after Stalin saw Lear become Stalin. It seems the Jew actor had been crushed to death by a truck."

EIGHT

WHERE THE KID COMPETES WITH THE PICK-UP-STICK KING OF GORI

FROM LEON'S NOTEBOOK:

ME: I envy you.

THE OLD MAN: Why in god's name would you envy me, kid?

ME: Hey, you get to live in a kind of fortress, for one thing. The windows are high in the walls, the front door is lined with sheets of metal bolted onto the inside, the spiral staircase is the only way in or out. When they're not playing chess, the four guards at the bottom of the staircase make sure nobody can get in to hurt you. I envy you being safe.

THE OLD MAN: Ha! All things considered, that's a laugh. I've never been safe. Not here. Not anywhere. Some egghead wrote something about nation-states having no permanent friends, only permanent interests. I have no permanent friends, only permanent enemies. As far back as I can remember there was always someone waiting to hurt me if I let down my guard for the blink of an eye.

ME: Did you ever? Let down your guard for the blink of an eye?

THE OLD MAN (*adrift in a memory*): Once. A lifetime ago. When I looked the other way, her fucking brother gave her a German pistol. She loaded it and murdered herself.

ME: How can you murder yourself? I don't understand.

THE OLD MAN: She shot a bullet into her chest where her heart would have been if she'd had a heart. The bitch murdered herself to punish me. And it worked—behind my back Stalin's kittens whispered that, figuratively speaking, it was me who had pulled the goddamn trigger.

THE NIGHT BEFORE I HAD FOUND THE OLD MAN in the bathroom—the door was wide open, which is how come I saw him when I passed—he was in his undershirt and standing in front of a medicine chest mirror and, tilting his head first one way and then the other, shaving with a straight-edged razor. The scraping sound of the blade against his skin reminded me of when I used to watch my father shave. The old man caught sight of me in the mirror. "Do you shave yet, kid?"

"I can tell you don't know much about raising kids. Hey, I'm only ten and a half and a bit. I'm too young to shave. I'm also too young to go to university or smoke cigarettes or masturbate or have sex."

He turned on the tap and rinsed the last of the shaving cream off his face, then dried himself with a towel as he came out of the bathroom. "Don't you know a joke when you hear one?"

It's true, I never knew when he was joking and when he wasn't, maybe because he sometimes said things that were insulting and, instead of apologizing, tried to pass them off as a joke. But that's a whole other story. I trailed after him, him struggling into his Army tunic as he made his way through the skating-rink living room into his office, walking more slowly, more painfully than I remembered, as though his joints ached. "I've been meaning to ask you something that's been on my mind," he said, lowering himself carefully into the seat behind the desk. He pushed his enormous revolver to one side and started tapping a cigarette on the desk to tamp down the tobacco.

"Ask, ask," I said, scraping over my seat to be closer to him. "I'm all ears."

He cleared his throat. "Do you think you'll remember me when I'm gone?"

"Where are you going?"

"Gone as in dead, kid. Will you remember the old man who gave you ice cream and taught you how to seduce girls when I'm dead?"

"You worried people won't remember you? You must have family. You must have friends. Hey, Valechka will remember you. And don't forget esteemed Comrade Stalin—how could he forget the hero of our glorious Revolution who helped him run the country?"

"I'm not asking about family or friends or Valechka or Stalin. I'm asking about you. Answer the fucking question. Will *you* remember me?"

"Sure I will. You can count on Leon to remember you. But I hope you're not planning on dying anytime soon."

"You never *plan* on dying, kid. It sneaks up on you on tiptoes—you don't hear it coming."

"Hey, I still don't know who you are? I know your mom called you Soso, I know your comrades back in Georgia called you Koba. Are you famous enough to have an obituary in *Pravda*?"

I could see the question tickled him. "Something modest on a back page is a possibility." And he laughed out loud as if what he said was hilarious. The laugh turned into a hacking cough, the cough into a wheeze. His good hand trembled as he aimed the flamethrower lighter at the end of the cigarette between his lips, then he inhaled deeply, which seemed to soothe him. "How about you, kid," he managed to say when he found his voice. "Are you afraid of dying?"

"I'm too young to be afraid of death."

"When do you plan to start thinking about it?"

"When I'm old. Say, thirty."

My *thirty* made him smile, though the smile still looked weird on his face. "Most kids your age are afraid of something—eating vegetables, ghosts, the dark," he said.

"Eating vegetables maybe. Ghosts, the dark, no way, especially when I have a flashlight. What about you? When you were my age were you afraid of the dark?"

"I have a hard time remembering back that far. When I was your age I was terrified of spiders."

"I love spiders."

"To this day I hate spiders. Even a tiny one on the wall near my bed panics me. I break into a cold sweat. Once I had to summon the chief of the guard to swat it. When I was a kid in Gori, my father used to come home drunk and become furious with me for something I'd done or something I should have done but didn't, and he'd lock me in the crawl space under the house for the night. It was swarming with spiders. I kept brushing them off my face and clothing until my sainted mother could pinch the key from his pocket and let me out. Sitting here with you now, remembering it, I can almost feel the spiders creeping on my skin."

"Besides spiders, what else do you hate?"

Sucking on his cigarette, Koba thought about this for a bit. "I hate an Italian by the name of Ratti, Ambrogio."

"Who is this Ratti, Ambrogio? And which one is his first name, Ratti or Ambrogio?"

"Ambrogio. He was a Pope. When you become Pope you abandon your old names and take on a new name. Ratti, Ambrogio became Pope Pius Roman Numeral something or other. Eleven, I think."

"So why do you hate Pope Roman Numeral Eleven?"

"In his infinite Papal wisdom, the son of a bitch decided Joseph Stalin was a greater threat to the world than Adolf Hitler. What a bonehead! Despite Catholicism and Communism being two isms struck from the same coin—they both demand unconditional cradle-to-grave submission— Roman Numeral Eleven loathed Communism more than fascism, this at a time when Hitler was setting up concentration camps and murdering German Communists while we were fighting the fascists in Spain. Listen, kid, in 1936 Roman Numeral Eleven offered a literary prize for the best anti-Communist novel. I wanted Stalin to offer a literary prize for the best anti-Catholic novel but his kittens talked him out of it. They were afraid it would antagonize American Catholics. Now that I think about it, I hate Roman Numeral Eleven more than I hate spiders."

LATER THAT NIGHT, AFTER I'D POLISHED OFF MY ice cream and the old man had drunk his second glass of warm milk and his ten drops of tincture of iodine, we got down on our knees on the floor of his office to play pick-up sticks. Hey, his idea, not mine. "I used to play all the time when I was your age," he told me. "I loved playing with my sons when they were growing up. Unfortunately they grew up and decided pick-up sticks wasn't dignified. When I was a kid there was a pick-up-stick tournament in Gori one summer. I came in first and was crowned pick-up-stick tsar of Gori. First prize was one of those thick leather gypsy belts set with colorful stones. My two revolvers were tucked into it when I robbed banks. After the tournament, my sainted mother was very proud of me but my father got pissed off when he noticed the knees of my city suit were dirty from kneeling. I could always tell when he was pissed at me. Looking me smack in the eye, he would slowly pull the belt out from the loops of his trousers."

I could see the old man getting ready to throw the sticks. "How come you go first?"

"We're playing with my sticks. In my office." He bunched the sticks, which were made of ivory, in his fist and then let them go. "Ah," he said, leaning down and harvesting the first four sticks that landed outside the pile and were a cinch. Squinting, he studied the lay of the land, then tried to take one that was straddling another, but his hand shook and the stick moved. Not wanting to humiliate him, I didn't say anything. Keeping his head down, he acted as if he hadn't noticed and continued playing. Thinking to flatter him out of his grumpy mood, I said, "I don't know if you're famous enough for *Pravda*, even on a back page, but I can tell you're pretty important."

"How can you tell?"

"The bodyguards downstairs. The rifles stacked against the wall. The way the Chief frisks me every time I come here, as if a kid might be hiding a gun."

"I'm important enough," he admitted, adding another ivory stick to his pile.

"Hey, Koba, can I ask you something?" He didn't say I couldn't so I worked up my courage and plowed ahead. "My best friend's father was shot as a British spy even though he didn't speak British. And my best friend's mother was arrested the same night my mom was arrested. If I give you their names, do you think you could raise the matter with esteemed Comrade Stalin?"

The old man sat back on his haunches, the pick-up sticks forgotten for the moment. "Let me stop you right there, kid. The security organs have the first and last word on who is and who isn't arrested, not Stalin. They make up the lists, they detain suspects and interrogate them, if there is evidence of treason they organize trials, if the defendant is found guilty by impartial NKVD troikas and sentenced to the highest measure of punishment, the security people execute the sentence."

"You already told me esteemed Comrade Stalin has nothing to do with the security organs. How many times are you going to repeat it?"

"As many times as it takes to instruct you. You need to get it into your thick skull, the guilt or innocence of a particular person is beside the point. As Stalin has been heard to say, *To make an omelette you are obliged to break eggs.* The important thing is that the trials and the occasional executions—in the case of your mothers, their arrests—serve as a warning to others who might be tempted to abandon the class struggle and give up on the construction of Communism. Think of it this way: The father of your friend, your mothers, are collateral casualties in the long struggle to perfect man and construct Communism in one country. Does my answer help you put the arrests into perspective?"

"Not really."

Shaking his head irritably, he leaned over the ivory sticks. "Enough questions for one night. Play the damn game."

NINE

WHERE ISABEAU SUSPECTS THE KID MAY HAVE LOST HIS MARBLES

FROM LEON'S NOTEBOOK:

THE OLD MAN: Here's what you need to know: All sex is rape. Do you understand the word *rape*, kid?

ME: It's when a man and a lady have sexual intercourse when the lady in question doesn't want to have sexual intercourse.

THE OLD MAN: You're close. Listen, even when you make love to a woman carefully and slowly, there is a built-in violence to fucking that qualifies as rape. Now that I think of it, relations between countries have a lot in common with sex. Things may appear to be going carefully and slowly but the reality is more violent: In a manner of speaking the imperialists are always trying to rape us. Roosevelt was out to rape Stalin at the Teheran conference in '43, again in Cairo that same year, again at Yalta in '45. By far the worst was Truman at Potsdam in '45. He was a tie salesman before he became president but he turned out to be the slickest anti-Soviet politician of them all—he invented the Cold War, he created their CIA, for Christ's sake. At Potsdam the tie salesman sidled up to Stalin and, casually puffing on a cigarette, told him the Americans had tested a secret weapon of unusual destructive force. Those were his exact words. The son of a bitch didn't say anything about it being an atomic bomb but of course we knew that. We probably knew the details of their uranium bomb and plutonium bomb before Truman was let in on the secret after Roosevelt's death. Our spies had been keeping us posted on what the Americans were up to in a remote corner of their New Mexico.

ME: Like, are you telling me our beloved Soviet Union actually has spies in the USA? Wow! If the unified field theory doesn't work out for me, being a spy in America would be my Plan B if I get to grow up.

THE OLD MAN: The business about the spies is a state secret. Keep it under your hat.

ME: Count on me, Koba.

THE OLD MAN: I do. Count on you, kid. There's nobody I count on more. (He looks away.) Present company excepted, there's nobody I count on at all.

SWEAR, CROSS MY HEART AND HOPE TO DIE, WE didn't know there were dead people living in the House on the Embankment, though I suppose if they're dead it's technically incorrect to say they're *living* here. Whatever. Ever since we deposited Raincoat's body in the minus-two swimming pool us kids had steered clear of the minus-two basement, one of the reasons being the smell of chlorine made my best friend, Leon, nauseous. But that didn't stop us from exploring the empty apartments off the secret passageways, at least the ones we could get into, in the hope of liberating tins of food or American board games or the occasional item of clothing like the fur mittens I wear on my feet when I go to sleep. As the people who once lived in these NKVD-sealed apartments no longer live in these apartments, we didn't think of it as stealing, it was more like *borrowing*, since except for the tin goods we had every intention of returning the stuff when the owners came back home—if the owners came back home. Late one night the four of us, the twins, Vladimir and Pavel, Leon and me—Zinaida didn't come with us because she was on the rag—we climbed up one flight to the fourth floor and began trying the doors to the secret rooms off the secret passageway. Pavel was all for forcing the locks but Leon and me, we talked him out of it because it would show the apartments had been broken into and we had enough worries already, what with the police having found a dead body in the minus-two swimming pool. Seven rooms into the passageway we came across an unlocked door. Vlad, who had the only flashlight, went in first and the rest of us followed, Indian file, each with a hand on the shoulder of the kid in front. The secret room turned out to be crawling with things you'd expect to find in one of the special state stores for VIPPs (Very Important Party People) where the wives arrive in government limousines to shop, namely cartons packed with cathode-ray radio tubes of various sizes and shapes, that and racks of women's high-heeled shoes that must have been manufactured in their Germany, as opposed to ours, because they looked very fashionable. I entertained the boys by fitting on a pair and, with Pavel's flashlight spotlighting me, flouncing across the room, swinging my ass and planting one foot directly in front of the other like those fashion models strutting down the runway in a Czech film I saw when my father was still alive. After a while Pavel aimed the beam of the flashlight on the door leading to the apartment. Leon and I exchanged looks. I nodded as if to say *Why not?* and he got up to try the knob. The door opened inward. On the apartment side we found shelves chock-full of detergents along with a collection of small statues of esteemed Comrade Stalin, the kind collective farm workers take back to their villages as souvenirs from Moscow. We were obviously in the apartment's laundry room, judging from the washer and dryer and the ironing board stacked with men's shirts waiting to be ironed. The twins were all for helping themselves to some shirts and calling it a night but Leon being Leon, he grabbed Pavel's flashlight and followed the beam into a bedroom with rumpled sheets on the mattress, as if it had been recently slept in. There were two empty valises open on the floor, and sunglasses and wristwatches and a woman's purse and what looked like car keys on the night table. Why would someone leave shirts and valises and eyeglasses and wristwatches and a purse and car keys behind if they were about to abandon their apartment? I was trying to come up with a rational explanation when Leon opened the next door and shot the beam of the flashlight into what turned out to be the dining room. I heard Leon gasp, I heard him slap the palm of his hand over his mouth to stifle a scream, I heard the stifled scream, I smelled the odor he must have been smelling, it was a hundred times awfuler than the chlorine from the minus-two swimming pool. Pavel and Vlad and me, we edged up to Leon in the doorway, which is when we saw what he was seeing.

How am I going to describe this without tears blurring the vision in my eyes? "For god's sake, don't look, Isabeau," Leon whispered when he realized I was next to him. Too late! What he saw, dear god, I still see even with my eyes closed. I pulled one of my executed father's hankies from the pocket of my sweater and clamped it over my nose and mouth. Too late! What I smelled that night, standing in the doorway of someone's dining room on the fourth floor of the House on the Embankment, is lodged in my nostrils for the rest of my life.

Okay. Here goes. There were two pretty old persons sitting at a long table, one on each end, a seven-branch silver candelabra with the candles burned down to their wicks between them, the woman was wearing a black lace evening dress, the man was wearing a black dinner jacket and had one of those embroidered Jewish yarmulkes on the back of his bald head. They had finished their meal and pushed away the plates filled with what was left of the chicken wings they'd eaten before slumping forward, forehead first, onto the Uzbek tablecloth like the one my mother used when she had company for supper. Two long-stemmed wineglasses were locked in the rigor-mortised fingers of the stone-dead persons, the wine that had been in them spilled on the tablecloth, it looked like dried blood to us kids, staring at the scene from the door. You didn't need to be a detective to figure out the two had been dead for days, maybe even weeks, judging from the stench. Pavel was the first to locate his vocal cords. "We need to get ourselves very far from here," he said in a flat voice. But Leon being Leon had other ideas. Without a word, skirting the table and the two persons who hadn't survived to digest their meal or finish the wine in their wineglasses, he headed for the apartment's front door. I could hear the chain safety lock being thrown and the door opening and I thought to myself, *Poor Leon has lost his marbles, he's going out the front door to tell the admiral in the lobby downstairs to call the police.* But poor Leon turned up a moment later, his face white as a ghost's, one bloodless lip chewing on the other bloodless lip as if he had discovered the secret of the spilled wine. Speaking super quietly so as not to wake the dead, he said, "There is no NKVD duct tape across the front door."

Pavel and Vlad didn't get it. "So?" they said in chorus.

Leon caught my eye and the solution to the mystery passed like an electric current between us. "I get it," I said. "It's as plain as the nose on your face, Pavel. These are Jewish persons. They knew the raincoats were concentrating on Jewish persons so they didn't hang around to get concentrated on."

Leon said, "They dressed up for the last supper and drank off their poisoned wine before the raincoats could arrest them."

Vladimir became agitated. "Which means they must have been enemies of the people! Hey, if they were going to be arrested they weren't innocent—"

Vladimir had started down a dead-end street but I couldn't resist nailing him to one of its walls. "My mother is not an enemy of the people," I informed him. "My father was not a Great Britain spy."

Pavel said, "Our mother and our big brother didn't throw cut glass into the bread dough at the bakery where they work."

Vladimir slapped his forehead. "Oh my god, what was I thinking of? Our father, when he was ambassador to Norway, didn't sell secret Soviet diplomatic telegrams to the American Central Intelligence Agency. Right, Pavel?"

"Right. Right. Totally right."

I remember Leon, looking older than ten and a half, or should I say talking older than ten and a half, saying, "I know for a fact my mom didn't plot to poison esteemed Comrade Stalin." We were all hypnotized by the bodies of the dead persons. "They were innocent like our parents," Leon whispered. "They are Jewish martyrs."

Pavel swallowed hard. "We still need to not be anywhere near here when they discover the dead persons." He turned to leave. We followed him through the laundry room, through the secret room, along the secret passageway to the staircase and down to the third floor. Before each of us went our own way we stood in a circle, our eight hands tightly clasped.

"We need to take a sacred oath never to breathe a word about what we saw to anybody," Pavel said.

"Not even Zinaida?" Vladimir asked.

"Especially Zinaida," I said. "She'll freak out. The last thing we need to deal with right now is a freaked-out Zinaida."

"I swear," Pavel said.

"I swear," Vladimir said.

"I swear," I said.

"Me too, I swear," Leon said. "Except I want to make an exception for the old man who lives over the airplane hangar. He needs to know what's happening in the country he helps run."

TEN

WHERE THE KID WORKS UP HIS NERVE TO SAY THE UNSAYABLE

FROM LEON'S NOTEBOOK:

THE OLD MAN: Stop me if you heard the story, kid. The tsar visits a hospital filled with the soldiers who were wounded fighting Napoleon. He asks four of them what they want as a reward for their service. The first soldier asks for a passport and a train ticket to Paris. The second asks for a farm and twenty cows. The third asks for a thousand rubles. The fourth soldier asks for a glass of vodka and a raw egg. After the tsar leaves, orderlies bring the fourth soldier a glass of vodka and a raw egg. He is the only one to get what he asked for. Can you identify the moral of the story?

ME: That's a piece of cake. The tsar was stingy.

THE OLD MAN (*snickering through his nose*): The moral is that the first three soldiers were greedy. You remind me of the fourth soldier, kid. You never want anything except a bowl of vanilla ice cream with chocolate sauce. Which is why you get a bowl of vanilla ice cream with chocolate sauce.

I FINALLY WORKED UP THE NERVE TO RAISE THE matter that was keeping me wide-awake nights. "What would you say if I told you I saw the dead bodies of two old Jewish persons who drank poison wine?"

The old man tapped one of his cigarettes on the desk to tamp down the tobacco, then, bending his head, he held President Roosevelt's flamethrower lighter to the end and lit it. He inhaled the smoke the way I couldn't and blew it out through his nostrils. "I'd say you have a lively imagination," he finally said. "I'd say you ought to think about writing novels if you grow up."

"If!"

"I meant when of course. When you grow up you could make up stories for a living." But I could tell from the way he eyed me he wasn't 100 percent sure I had made up the story. "So what made you think they were Yids?" I remember him asking.

"Yids is a bad word. You should say Israelites. You should say Jews."

"Watch yourself, kid. You're not my fucking conscience. I've gotten along very well, thank you, without one up to now."

You know how sometimes your ears hear words come out your mouth before you've had a chance to think of what to say and your brain, hearing these words, discovers what you think. Well, that's what happened to me, watching this grumpy old man with iodine breath, what hair he still had on his head drifting off in every direction, puffing away on one of his Herzegovina Flors as if his life depended on it, which for all I know it did. Hey, consider the possibility it was the cigarette that kept him inhaling and exhaling, which, when you think about it, has a lot in common with breathing in and out. Waving my fingers to scatter the foul-smelling smoke, I heard myself say, "Maybe not having a conscience is your problem."

The old man concentrated on his cigarette. "So where did you see these dead Yids, kid?"

"In an apartment in the building where I live."

His nostrils twitched as if they had sniffed out a contradiction. "How could you know they were Yids if they were dead and didn't speak to you in Yiddish?"

I described the seven-branch candelabra. I described the yarmulke on the bald head of the man.

The ash on his cigarette grew so long it looked as if it was defying gravity—although speaking as a ten-and-a-half-year-old apprentice physicist, I'm not convinced gravity can be defied—but the old man, tangled up in his thoughts, didn't seem to notice. "I told you I have no connection with the security organs," he said. "But if the Yids killed themselves before they could be arrested, it must mean they were guilty of something that would have come out once they'd been arrested."

I need to describe the scene. It's almost as if there were three of us in the room, the old man holding fort behind his gigantic desk absently fingering his enormous revolver, the ten-and-a-half-year-old kid balanced nervously on the edge of the chair staring at him—and yours truly, the hypothetical authorized biographer, listening to what they said to each other, back and forth, my head turning from one to the other as if I was watching a hockey match. Maybe it was the double suicide in the House on the Embankment, maybe it was Anastasia Andreevna Rozental confessing to crimes she hadn't committed, maybe it was both that pushed Leon to utter words that in Soviet Russia were unutterable.

"What they were guilty of was being Jewish."

The remark startled the old man. I saw him hesitate. "I give you credit," I heard him say, his voice ominously muffled. "You've got balls."

"Hey, I'm only saying out loud what people whisper."

The old man was growing sorer by the second. "The Soviet Union does not discriminate against its citizens who, through no fault of their own, have the misfortune to be Yids."

Speaking as the hypothetical authorized biographer, I could tell the kid couldn't believe his ears. This is what, to my amazement, I heard him say: "Remember the first time I came up here, Koba? You asked me to name three reasons why you should talk to me. I gave you two, I said I was working on the third. Well, I just discovered my third. It was right in front of my nose but it was so close I couldn't see it. Even if I knew who you were, which I don't, I wouldn't be afraid of you because *you're not scary*. You're just a bitter old man with bad teeth and bad breath who farts a lot and says the first dumb thing that comes into his head."

The cigarette had burned down so far it singed the old man's lip. He yelped in pain and, plucking it from his mouth, stubbed it out in the artillery shell overflowing with cigarette ends. "And here I thought you were a smart-ass," I heard him say. "My mistake. You're deceiving yourself, kid, if you think someone who helps Stalin run the country says the first thing that comes into his head. I weigh my words, which is why people pay attention to them. There is no daylight between what I say and what Stalin thinks. I read the reports that Stalin reads, I am familiar with the juicy details the organs provide in these reports, I sign off on the decisions Stalin makes, I add my *za* to Stalin's on the upper right-hand corner of pages filled with endless lists of names." He stabbed his good hand into one of the desk drawers and dragged out a gunmetal attaché case like the one my father kept his atomic secrets in. He produced a key at the end of a long chain attached to his belt and, after several stabs managed to get the key in and open the lock, then riffled angrily through a thick wad of papers with red sealing wax on them until he found the one he was looking for. "This, this one here, it proves I'm not the ogre you make me out to be. The anti-Soviet elements that wound up in Siberia weren't arrested because they were of a particular religious persuasion. Our CheKists are fucking professionals—they arrested individuals of a particular *political* persuasion, they arrested *enemies of the people*, not Yids. They shot *enemies of the people*, not Yids, for Christ's sake, though some of the enemies of the people through no fault of their own may have been Yids." He thwacked the sheet of paper furiously with the palm of his hand. "Here. Read it yourself if it will make you less stupid. NKVD Order Number 00447 of July 1937. There is no mention of Yids, none, not one, only a list, region by region, of kulaks to be shot or sent off to Siberia. In the Odessa region, a thousand shot, thirty-five hundred deported. No mention of Yids. None. Here's another. Ethnic Germans and Poles who might be tempted to collaborate with an invading army were rounded up and sentenced to *ten years without right of correspondence*, which as every idiot knows is CheKist jargon for HMP, *highest measure of punishment*. Again, there's no mention of Yids. None. Here, look, the organs recorded 681,691 executions in 1937, all *kulaks* or anti-Soviet elements. Not a single word about Yids. Not one. None. It goes without saying but I'll say it so you don't go back home dumber than when you showed up tonight: Stalin had no role in any of this. He was a bystander. It was the organs that decided who was and who wasn't an enemy of the people. The capitalist press pretends that fifteen hundred were shot every day. It's not impossible. I can't say one way or the other. But if fifteen hundred were shot every day, make room for this information in your kid-sized brain"—he looked up from the paper, his eyes bloodshot with rage, and shouted out—*"they weren't shot because they were Yids!"*

The kid, alarmed, leaped to his feet so suddenly his chair crashed over backward to the floor.

Valechka appeared out of nowhere. She came up behind the old man and began massaging his forehead with her fingertips. "Calm yourself, Joseph. You're frightening the boy."

"The little prick needs to be frightened." He pried Valechka's hands away from his head. "Fuck him, he doesn't realize who he's talking to if he can say the things he said."

"He's only a child, Joseph."

The old man was ranting now. "His father was the Yid scientist Rozental who sabotaged our first chain reaction. His mother is a Yid who confessed to conspiring with Kremlin doctors to murder Stalin. The kid's a fucking Yid. If he grows up—*if* he grows up!—he's going to turn out like all the Yids, an enemy of the people, a member of the fifth column waiting to stab us in the back the instant the American tie salesman Truman attacks the Soviet Union. Mark my words, Valechka, the *child*, as you call him, is sucking up to power. Like the other Yids I've had to deal with, he expects something in return. Trotsky, Kaganovitch, Zinoviev, Kamenev, Molotov's Yid wife Polina, Yakov's Yid wife Yulia, the circumcised prick Svetlana hitched herself to, they all sucked up to me, they all expected something in return. Don't stand there with your mouth drooping open, kid, spit it out, tell me what you want besides vanilla ice cream covered in chocolate sauce."

And I heard this voice that sounded an awful lot like mine say, "I'm too young to drink vodka. I'll settle for the raw egg and my mom coming home from jail."

The old man was trembling with rage. "Get the fuck out," he screamed. "Get out before I throw you out. Get out and don't come back."

"Maybe you should leave, Leon," Valechka said. Plainly shaken, she made her way around the desk and took the kid's hand and pulled him toward the door. "We're going to the Near Dacha for three weeks," she whispered. "He will have forgotten all about this by then. He enjoys your company. Come back in three weeks."

"The Near Dacha is esteemed Comrade Stalin's dacha!" the kid remembered, but Valechka, watching anxiously over her shoulder as the old man fumbled wildly through the gunmetal attaché case, wasn't hanging on his every word.

ELEVEN

WHERE THE KID DECIDES TO SWALLOW HIS PRIDE

FROM LEON'S NOTEBOOK:

ME: Do you have regrets?

THE OLD MAN: Dumb question. At my age everyone has regrets.

ME: Let the record show you're not answering my dumb question.

THE OLD MAN: What are you, a lawyer?

ME: I heard a lawyer say that in a movie.

THE OLD MAN: How about you, kid. What do you regret at the ripe age of ten and a half?

ME: I regret they used graphite instead of heavy water to slow down the chain reaction. I regret being trapped in kidhood. I regret my best friend Isabeau doesn't have breasts.

THE OLD MAN (*after a moment*): I regret growing old.

ME: Old age is not for the weak of heart.

THE OLD MAN: You can say that again.

ME: Old age is not for the weak of heart.

THE OLD MAN: I didn't mean literally, for Christ's sake.

ME: Are you afraid of dying?

THE OLD MAN: I'm not thrilled about dying. But I'm more afraid of being ignored, I'm more afraid of being forgotten. The thing I'm most afraid of is being condemned to the dustbin of history.

HEY, SINCE I STILL HAD NO IDEA WHO HE WAS, except when he loses his temper there was no reason for me to be afraid of him. But given how antique he was and how mean he could be and how his breath reeked of iodine and Herzegovina Flors, not to mention his disgusting attitude toward Jewish people like my mom and dad and me, I made up my mind to never ever go back to that Little Corner of his. And when Leon makes up his mind about something you can bet . . . well, you can bet when he calms down he'll ask himself what his father would do in this situation, at which point he'll re-evaluate, he'll weigh the pros and cons, he'll at least toy with the idea of following Valechka's instinct as opposed to his own. Look, if, as she told me that awful night in the apartment above the hangar, the old man really enjoyed my company, if he really will have forgotten about the outburst which, let's face it, I provoked, well, what did I have to lose except my pride? And what was pride compared to two heaping scoops of vanilla ice cream smothered in chocolate sauce? Or the authorized biography I could write about the old man if it turns out he is important enough to be mentioned in *Pravda*, even on a back page.

Which more or less explains how, three weeks to the day after the old man's Etna-esque eruption, I made my way down to the minus-three basement in the House on the Embankment and headed into the tunnel. Little had changed since my first treks under the river Styx. Pipes fitted with nozzles still spit thin jets of steam into the moist air, warming the tunnel. Dozens and dozens of men, snugging in filthy Army greatcoats, still camped on ledges or in nooks or on piled-up wooden packing crates, but I'd been through the tunnel so many times I knew how to dodge the hands that reached out to snag my ankle as I splashed through the film of water on the brick floor. I ducked into the narrow tunnel that branched off from the main tunnel and climbed the not-so-rusted steel staircase at least three floors up, maybe four, and then squeezed sideways through the narrow wooden door into the humongous airplane hangar big enough to hold two of those big Soviet bombers. Unlike my previous visits, the giant chandeliers dangling from the funny-shaped ceiling were blazing with light. The hangar itself was deserted except for six military officers in dress blue uniforms complete with swords standing at a side table helping themselves to coffee from an urn. They were obviously some kind of honor guard taking a break from guarding whatever they were supposed to be honoring by guarding. Then I noticed what they must have been honor guarding. Smack in the middle of the hangar was a raised platform with, get this, an open coffin on it. As I drew nearer I could hear someone sobbing softly. When I edged around the foot of the coffin I saw it was Valechka. She was kneeling on the platform next to the coffin; she was gazing into it and crying her heart out.

I climbed onto the platform and put a hand on her shoulder to console her in her misery. Only then did I glance into the coffin and notice that the inquiline inside was the old man. The thought flashed through my head that he was sound asleep on a bed of soft white satin and I wondered why he'd decided to sleep down here in the hangar instead of on the big comfortable bed in his apartment above it. Crazy as this sounds, he reminded me of my father's Swiss pocket watch that had been overwound and stopped ticking. I'm embarrassed to admit it took an eternity of seconds for my brain to process the information working its way up from my eyes, to realize *Koba had stopped ticking*—he wasn't *sleeping* in the coffin, he was dead as a doornail in the coffin. Funnily, in death he looked younger than I remembered. For starters he had more hair, or maybe it had been combed to make it look as if he had more hair. His cheeks were a healthy-looking ruddy. The pockmarks on his face, the bags under his eyes, and the garlic cloves he wore around his neck had all vanished. A pained smile sat frozen on his rouged lips, knowing him he would have summoned it to salute the angel of death. His fingers were overlapping on the chest of a spanking grey military tunic crawling with medals, which made it impossible to notice that one arm was shorter than the other.

"Oh, Leon," Valechka exclaimed, looking up at me, "you came back. He would have liked that."

I could see the honor guard eyeing me. "It's alright," she called over to them through her tears. "The child is with me."

"What happened?" I asked in a whisper.

"He had a stroke in the Near Dacha. By the time they could fetch a doctor from Moscow, there was nothing to be done but watch the life drain out of him."

"I'm sorry for your loss," I murmured.

"Me too, Leon, I'm sorry for my loss. I was only his housekeeper, and you're the first one to give a damn about *my* loss. Most of the people he came in contact with, especially the ones he called kittens, were afraid of him. They mistook him for a hard-hearted old man, if they had looked under the surface they would have seen he was just a brokenhearted old man. He didn't feel a connection to his own children, to his children's children." Valechka pulled a handkerchief from a pocket and blew her nose loudly into it. "He was very lonely in that suffocating apartment of his upstairs, which is why he valued your company. You broke through this wall of loneliness. You were one of his rare contacts with the outside world, the *real* world. He didn't play a role with you. He didn't have to. He could be himself."

"What's going to happen to him now?"

"Why, he'll lie in state here for a day or two so the kittens can shed crocodile tears when they pay their last respects. Then they will surely organize a grandiose funeral. You can count on them to send our Georgian peasant off in vulgar style."

"Do you think they'll mention his passing in *Pravda*, even on a back page?"

Valechka looked quickly at me as if she thought I might be making a joke to cheer her up. When she saw I was dead serious, she said "Dear Leon, you really didn't know who he was, did you? That's probably why you got along so well. Yes, yes, there's a good chance there will be a mention of his passing in *Pravda*. If it's a slow day, it might even make the front page."

TWELVE

WHERE THE KID APPLIES HEISENBERG'S UNCERTAINTY PRINCIPLE TO LIFE

FROM LEON'S NOTEBOOK:

THE OLD MAN: Listen, kid, if you've done what I suggested and written down all the things I told you, all my stories, all my regrets, all my complaints, all my trepidations, you'd have my authorized biography.

ME: How can I write your biography, authorized or otherwise, if I don't even know your name?

THE OLD MAN: *If* you grow up—okay, okay, *when* you grow up—you will.

S O I WAS STRETCHED OUT ON THE COT IN MY secret room, rereading the chapter in Isaac Newton's *Philosophiæ Naturalis Principia Mathematica* my dad had marked in red before he died of radiation poisoning, when I heard a scuffing inside our apartment. Worried sick the raincoats had come back to search the rooms again—who knows what evidence they would plant and pretend to find—I scampered up onto the three-step stepladder to peer through the slit that, on the apartment side, looked like a crack in the plaster. I could make out an old lady shuffling into the living room. I was relieved not to discover a man wearing a raincoat even though it wasn't raining out. Still, I was confused because I'd never seen the lady before in my life. Isabeau told me they sometimes assigned new tenants to live in the apartments of arrested people and I figured that must be what's happening. How else could the lady have gotten a key to the front door, how else, even if she somehow got hold of the key, would she have dared to cut the NKVD duct tape sealing off the apartment? The lady stood for a long time looking around the room, then tried to shrug off her overcoat, but she had trouble getting her arms out of the sleeves and gave up, collapsing onto the couch. Watching her run her fingers over the seedy cushions on our couch almost as if she recognized them, the old lady suddenly seemed vaguely familiar. She reminded me of someone I'd seen before—but where? And then, boy oh boy, I saw she was staring up at the crack in the living room plaster, tears trickling down her cheeks, a half-peeved half smile on her swollen lips. "Mom," I whispered to myself and in my excitement I almost toppled off the ladder. *"Mom!"* I screamed as I pushed through the secret door into the apartment and fell into her arms. I'm not discomforted to report that the waterfall of tears spilling from my eyes almost blinded me. "Be careful, Leon," I heard her say in a husky voice, "I have broken ribs, a dislocated shoulder." Falling quickly back onto my butt, I saw she was wearing the same flat-soled white shoes she had on the night of her arrest. Looking up into her face, I noticed the bruises on her cheekbones, the black eye, the missing teeth. "What did they do to you, Mom?" I cried. She patted my head. "I was terrified you wouldn't be here," she murmured. I grabbed hold of one of her hands—two of her fingers were horribly swollen. Hey, you want to hear something funny? She wound up comforting me, not me, her. "Don't be alarmed, my darling Leon," she whispered. "Keep in mind I am a doctor. The broken fingers, the cracked ribs, the dislocated shoulder, they will all mend with time. The important thing is I've come home and found the man of the family alive and well."

I remembered something the old man told me during one of our confabulations. "I need to ask you something, Mom."

"Ask, ask."

"Is it true you confessed?"

She tried to smile that half smile of hers, the one she owned the patent to, and winced from the soreness in her bruised face. "When I couldn't bear the pain I confessed to stop them from beating me."

"Oh, Mom, I absolutely knew you were innocent! I was positive you would never ever try to poison esteemed Comrade Stalin. Hey, you were lucky they let you go after you confessed."

I remember my mom speaking so softly I had to strain to catch her words. "It wasn't luck, Leon," is what I think she said. "The interrogator showed me a handwritten note on Kremlin stationery—it mentioned me by name, Anastasia Andreevna Rozental, it was signed but the signature was unreadable, the word *za* was scrawled in red ink in the upper right-hand corner, it instructed the organs to release me if I was still alive. The guards dragged me upstairs to the infirmary and permitted me to wash and gave me new underwear and put me to bed in a real bed with clean sheets. I slept for three days and three nights." I remember her almost smiling again despite the pain it caused her. "During the endless interrogations when they were trying to beat a confession out of me, I never dared hope there might be someone in the Kremlin who remembered my name."

Looking over my own shoulder at the story I'm telling, I can report that this was the instant the kopek dropped. How could I not have seen what was right in front of my nose, how could I not have recognized the old man who scratched *za* in red ink on the upper right-hand corner of files, how could I not have comprehended whom I'd been confabulating with when I heard Koba ranting into the enormous black telephone on his desk. *"No, I am not giving instructions, I am merely passing on a casual comment of Stalin's. It's up to you to figure out what he meant. It is up to you to figure out what to do."*

My tears drenched the back of my mom's hand, which I was holding. "Koba remembered your name," I breathed.

My mom looked at me funnily. "Who is Koba?" she asked.

"He's an old man with bullfrog eyes and iodine breath and a mustache that looks an awful lot like esteemed Comrade Stalin's," I said. And I carefully buried my bursting brain in my mom's aching lap.

The twins, Vladimir and Pavel, and their half sister Zinaida found their mother dazed and wandering in the hallway two or three days later. She couldn't recall which apartment she lived in, she remembered she had children but she didn't remember how many or their names. Their father never did come back and they were never able to find out, despite appeals to the organs, what happened to him. When anybody asked Pavel about his father, he would say he was missing in action, as if he was a collateral casualty of war, which, you'll remember, is what the old man called it.

Isabeau's mother returned home a week after my mom and in pretty much the same shape. One day later Isabeau came to say goodbye forever. True to her promise, they had packed their valises and were going off to live in Uzbekistan in the hope of getting as far away from the NKVD raincoats as possible. "With any luck," Isabeau told me, "out of sight will be out of mind." I remember she looked at me weirdly. "I'm still not sure what to think about this old man of yours," she admitted. "I've read your notebook but the things he says don't always hold water."

"It doesn't matter," I said.

"It does matter," she insisted, "but I'm not sure why. What am I missing?"

"Please don't go to Uzbekistan, Isabeau."

"I don't have a choice."

"I'm pretty sure I love you," I whispered in panic.

"I'm pretty sure I love you back, Leon. Not to worry. Absence is supposed to make the heart grow fonder."

"Who says?"

"Me. I. Whichever."

I'm not discomfited to report that Isabeau hit me with one of her scrumptiously naughty smiles just before she kissed me again—again on the lips.

I like to think our hearts did grow fonder—but in the end Isabeau's absence weighed more than Koba's Soviet State with its planes and tanks and ships and trains and tractors and trucks. After a while I found I couldn't reproduce her mocking laughter echoing across the minus-two swimming pool in my mind's ear. After another while I couldn't even reproduce her scrumptiously naughty smile in my mind's eye. You can bet we kept in touch, Isabeau and me, writing rambling letters on onionskin airmail paper, for the better part of three years, which was more or less when the letters began to peter out. It was as much my fault as hers—I had a lot on my dance card when, to my surprise, I actually lived long enough to be a teenager. Here is what was on my dance card: I became the youngest kid ever to be admitted to Moscow State University. I'm in my third year now and I'm already working on my senior thesis, which deals with the interaction of subatomic particles in the light of Heisenberg's uncertainty principle. (*Mea culpa*: It was me who couldn't resist scribbling *Werner Heisenberg, make up your mind!* on the wall over the urinal in the men's toilet of the physics department.) When I'm not studying particle physics I audit a course on English lyric poetry, partly because I actually like English lyric poetry, partly because the professor reading English poetry with a thick Russian accent tends to attract the cutest girls. I feel a special affinity for Robert Herrick of *gather ye rosebuds* fame. Hey, I'm following his advice and gathering rosebuds where I find them, which at the moment happens to be Moscow State University. Recently I began composing my own poems, which I have been known to read out to the occasional girlfriend, averting my eyes, to use Koba's formula, so she won't see I'm stretching the truth when I swear I wrote it for her.

I need to confess here: There's a downside to my status as a kid prodigy. Being the only unapologetic Stalinist in the room at university bull sessions can be discomforting nowadays, I'm talking 1956, what with Nikita what's-his-name having openly denounced—for *criminal* wrongdoings, no less!—the late, and until the day before yesterday, the lamented general secretary. Me being the only one in the room who can claim to have an opinion based on stuff he heard from the horse's mouth, I resist the opportunists who, to promote their own careers, would persuade us that esteemed Comrade Stalin was Lucifer incarnate. Like, it's not as if the dude who ruled Russia for thirty years was some medieval priest selling indulgences for sins people hoped to commit. He had bigger fish to fry. My mom's ordeal notwithstanding, I seriously believe esteemed Comrade Stalin gets credit for the survival of the Soviet Union—I'm talking crash industrialization (which wouldn't have been possible without crash collectivization), I'm talking the glorious Red Army raising our Russian hammer and sickle over the Reichstag in Berlin and the awful Adolf Hitler dead and cremated in his bunker. My mom's ordeal notwithstanding, I seriously believe esteemed Comrade Stalin did the things he did in order to make Russia great again.

My mom's ordeal *withstanding*, I know for a fact she doesn't swallow my line about esteemed Comrade Stalin making Russia great again. Being a doctor, she seems to have diagnosed esteemed Comrade Stalin and our glorious Russia with terminal inferiority complex. But that's a whole other story.

Or, hey, is it?

As for yours truly, I'm thrilled to be a student in my country's oldest university. Going to school every morning in the colossal wedding-cake skyscraper esteemed Comrade Stalin built on Sparrow Hills, I pinch myself to be sure I'm not dreaming. (My late and totally lamented father, who you'll remember wore his sweaters outside in, always called Lenin Hills by its old Russian name, which happens to be Sparrow Hills. I need to figure out what my dad knew that I didn't about the future that needs work.) To answer your question before you ask it, I think about the old man living above the hangar all the time. There are moments when I imagine I imagined him. Most of the time, though, this vintage Georgian wine bottled in Moscow, as he put it, is scarily real nightmare fodder. *Organize the disorder, disorder the organized!* Wow! Like, I owe him big time for his *za* in red ink that got my mother out of prison. Maybe, hey, maybe the *za* was his way of saying he regretted losing his temper that awful night he threw me out of his apartment. Maybe it was a lonely old man's way of saying he appreciated the confabulations with a kid who wasn't afraid of him. Either or. All things considered, I still can't decide whether Koba was hard-hearted or brokenhearted. Or half-hearted. Or—when I remember his rant about, excuse the expression, *Yids*—heartbreakingly heartless. You wouldn't be wrong to call this Rozental's uncertainty principle. (*Mea maxima culpa*: I scribbled a second graffito on the wall over the urinal: *Leon Rozental, make up your mind!*) As I told Isabeau in one of my last letters to her, I still hear the grumpy voice of this frightened old man in my mind's ear. *Nobody is innocent!* I see now he must have been including himself, though, hey, consider the possibility—consider the probability!—even if he didn't finish up innocent, he must have started out innocent in the previous incarnation we call childhood.

FROM LEON'S NOTEBOOK:

THE OLD MAN: I wasn't all that much older than you when I had this major event in my life. I was still living with my parents in Gori at the time. My face was scarred from the smallpox—the local girls nicknamed me *Chophura*, Georgian for *pockmarked*—which made me very unsure of myself with members of the weaker sex. There was this one girl—I never forgot her name, it was Fazu—she was fifteen and sort of pretty if you needed eyeglasses but weren't wearing them. She had a shy way of smiling at me when I passed her in the street. One night I invited her down to the Liakhva to watch the full moon rising over the mountains across the river. Slipping my arm around her waist, with the palm of my hand on her hip, I remember telling myself, *Iosif, this is as good as it gets, don't expect better*, and I spit one of my poems across the river at the mountains.

I'll bare my breast to you, extend
My arm in joyous greeting, too.
My spirit trembling, once again
I glimpse before me the bright moon.

I wrote it long before I took Fazu down to the river but, averting my eyes so she wouldn't see I was stretching the truth, I swore I'd written it for her.

ME: And then?

THE OLD MAN: What makes you think there's an *and then*?

ME: Come clean, Koba. Knowing you, knowing you wrote love poems to sweet talk girls into your bed, there has got to be an *and then*. Why tell me the story otherwise?

THE OLD MAN: And then, if you must know, Christ, I screwed up my courage and I . . . what the hell, I kissed her. Smack on the lips.

ME (*pissed that I'd been cheated out of a juicy detail*): That's it! That's your *and then*?

THE OLD MAN (*laughing under his revolting iodine breath*): That's it, kid.